Maya Blake's hopes of becoming a writer were born when she picked up her first romance at thirteen. Little did she know her dream would come true! Does she still pinch herself every now and then to make sure it's not a dream? Yes, she does! Feel free to pinch her, too, via Twitter, Facebook or Goodreads! Happy reading!

Books by Maya Blake

Mills & Boon Modern Romance

Signed Over to Santino
A Diamond Deal with the Greek
A Marriage Fit for a Sinner
Married for the Prince's Convenience
Innocent in His Diamonds
His Ultimate Prize
Marriage Made of Secrets
The Sinful Art of Revenge
The Price of Success

Secret Heirs of Billionaires

Brunetti's Secret Son

The Untameable Greeks

What the Greek's Money Can't Buy
What the Greek Can't Resist
What the Greek Wants Most

The 21st Century Gentleman's Club

The Ultimate Playboy

Visit the Author Profile page
at millsandboon.co.uk for more titles.

To my readers and happy-ever-after lovers everywhere.
This one's for you.

THE DI SIONE
SECRET BABY

BY
MAYA BLAKE

MILLS &
BOON

First Published in Great Britain 2016
By Mills & Boon, an imprint of HarperCollins*Publishers*
1 London Bridge Street, London, SE1 9GF

© 2016 Harlequin Books S.A.

Special thanks and acknowledgement are given to Maya Blake
for her contribution to The Billionaire's Legacy series.

ISBN: 978-0-263-91631-7

Our policy is to use papers that are natural, renewable and recyclable
products and made from wood grown in sustainable forests. The logging
and manufacturing processes conform to the legal environmental
regulations of the country of origin.

Printed and bound in Spain
by CPI, Barcelona

'This is how you want to make amends?' Rahim enquired, his voice gravel-hoarse with arousal. 'Think carefully before you answer, *habibi*. Because once you answer in the affirmative, once I have you in my bed, there will be no going back.'

Allegra wanted to tell him that she knew she'd already burned bridges where he was concerned. From the moment they'd touched she'd known Rahim Al-Hadi had an inexplicable power over her. Allegra knew it was why she'd reacted so uncharacteristically strongly to him. Whether she wanted him to matter or not, Rahim spoke to a need in her soul she couldn't deny.

And right here, right now, she didn't want to.

'Yes,' she whispered. Then in a stronger voice, because her very soul demanded it, she repeated, 'Yes, I want this.'

The Billionaire's Legacy

A search for truth and the promise of passion!

For nearly sixty years
Italian billionaire Giovanni Di Sione has kept
a shocking secret. Now, nearing the end of his days,
he wants his grandchildren to know their true heritage.

He sends them each on a journey to find his
'Lost Mistresses'—a collection of love tokens
and the only remaining evidence of his lost identity,
his lost history…his lost love.

With each item collected the Di Sione siblings take one
step closer to the truth…and embark on a passionate
journey that none could have expected!

Find out what happens in

The Billionaire's Legacy

Di Sione's Innocent Conquest by Carol Marinelli

The Di Sione Secret Baby by Maya Blake

To Blackmail a Di Sione by Rachael Thomas

The Return of the Di Sione Wife by Caitlin Crews

Di Sione's Virgin Mistress by Sharon Kendrick

A Di Sione for the Greek's Pleasure by Kate Hewitt

A Deal for the Di Sione Ring by Jennifer Hayward

The Last Di Sione Claims His Prize by Maisey Yates

Collect all 8 volumes!

CHAPTER ONE

ALLEGRA LOOKED UP and smiled at the flight attendant. With a slight shake of her head and a numb smile, she refused the proffered glass of champagne. Thankfully, the first-class cabin was nearly empty. No one could witness her shock or deep worry. No one could tell she still reeled from the news her brother Matteo had delivered two days ago.

How could Grandfather have kept the true extent of his illness from her? She'd known he was undergoing tests since doctors suspected his leukaemia had returned, but he'd brushed her off when she'd asked him about his prognosis two months ago. Now she knew.

One year to live.

Her heart clenched. It was impossible to believe the man who'd always seemed larger than life wouldn't be here for Christmas next year. Tears welled in her eyes. She quickly dashed them away as she sensed the effervescent flight attendant returning. She couldn't lose her composure. The world was watching. And these days, with technology streamed faster than the speed of light, maintaining the right appearances at all times was even more paramount.

For she was Allegra Di Sione, oldest granddaughter of one of the most powerful men in the world. She was also the face of the Di Sione Foundation, a charity she'd dedicated her life to. A full-time job she was more than happy to immerse herself in, even if it meant embracing a life that more often than not felt desperately lonely.

Shaking herself free of the self-involved thoughts, she glanced out the window as the plane left its berth at Dubai International Airport and slotted into place on the runway.

The early May sunshine was dazzling. Almost as dazzling as the wealthy guests and stunning success her foundation's latest gala had been. Her well-oiled charity team assured her it was their best yet, with almost double the amount raised last year, but Allegra, as proud as she was of her achievements, couldn't dwell on that now.

Not when Matteo's words continued to spin in her head. Besides the news of the old man's declining health, her brother had dropped another bombshell.

Grandfather's little fable wasn't a fable at all, if Matteo was to be believed.

For as long as she could remember, she'd thrilled to the story about her grandfather's Lost Mistresses. At one time she'd even wondered if her grandfather had led as decadent a life as her parents to possess such wild stories. She'd discarded that idea because she knew her grandfather had remained devoted to her grandmother until she'd died. His integrity was one of the many stalwarts she'd tried to emulate. Besides that, building the Di Sione fortune had been his number-one priority.

Discovering that the Lost Mistresses held real-life meaning, however, was one reality she hadn't been prepared for. Because why would her grandfather task her brother with retrieving a long-lost necklace on a whim?

As for the look in Matteo's eyes when he'd told her to return home without delay...

Allegra sucked in a deep breath as the plane thundered down the runway and lifted into the arid desert sky.

She'd faced losing her parents in the most horrific, media-guzzling way when she was six years old. She'd smothered her own pain in order to be there for her six siblings, despite desperately missing the mother whose love had been as volatile as it'd been all-encompassing.

Whatever her grandfather had to tell her, she would face it.

Despite the bracing pep talk she'd given herself all through her flight, Allegra couldn't stop the full-body tremble as the town car turned into the long driveway that led to the place she called home. She kept a three-bedroom condo on the Upper East Side in New York City, but the Di Sione family estate in Long Island where she'd grown up with her brothers and sisters was her true home.

As with most homes, the memories that came with it were bittersweet, although in the case of her siblings and her, they were more bitter than sweet. Allegra couldn't stop her gaze from darting up the northwest corner of the stunning sprawling mansion that was the Di Sione estate. Cultivated lawns surrounded it with just a glimpse of Long Island Sound further beyond.

It was where she'd been brought after the night she'd stood at her parents' home, watching her mother and father enact what was to be their ultimate screaming drug-fuelled row.

Two hours after that harrowing performance, a single, ominous police cruiser had arrived; an officer had stepped out, and, with a few words, turned her and her siblings into orphans.

Enough.

Allegra pushed the bad memory to the back of her mind, and exited the car.

The double doors opened and Alma, the housekeeper, who'd been part of their family for longer than Allegra could remember, stepped out. Although the elderly Italian woman's smile was huge and welcoming as always,

Allegra spotted the worry in her soft brown eyes and in the furtive wring of her hands.

'Miss Allegra, it has been too long,' she murmured when Allegra stepped into the vast marble-floored hallway.

Allegra nodded, but her gaze was already seeking the familiar figure of her grandfather, her heart slamming against her ribs anew at the thought of him being taken away from them. 'Where is he? *How* is he?' she asked.

Alma's smile dimmed further. 'The doctor has advised bed rest, but Signor Giovanni…he insists he's having a good day. He's sitting outside, in his favourite spot.'

Allegra turned away from the imposing wrought-iron staircase that soared three floors, intending to head for the west wing of the villa, to the place where her grandfather had taken his breakfast for as long as she could remember.

'Allegra?'

She stopped and turned back to Alma. The distress on her slightly wrinkled face was pronounced enough to send a cold shiver down Allegra's spine.

She hadn't doubted her brother for one moment, but truth be told, Matteo had been a little preoccupied with the woman he'd attended the foundation gala with. In a secret part of her, Allegra had hoped he was exaggerating the severity of the situation when he'd spoken to her in Dubai.

The expression on the housekeeper's face now confirmed to Allegra that Matteo hadn't been exaggerating.

'He's not as he was the last time you saw him. Be prepared.'

Mouth dry, Allegra nodded, ran her damp palms on her knee-length navy blue linen dress and continued down the west hallway, neither seeing nor appreciating the light that filtered through tall windows onto priceless works of art that graced the walls.

All she cared about was making it to the end of the corridor, and through the double French doors that led to the pillared terrace.

Be prepared.

Despite the warning, Allegra gasped as she stepped out into the sunshine. She'd expected her grandfather to be sitting in his favourite outdoor armchair. The sight of the bed, rigged with what looked like an oxygen canister, was such a shock to her system she froze in the doorway.

In the bed, her grandfather lay, with folds of cashmere blankets tucked up to his waist. His chest rose and fell in shallow breaths and his lids were lowered. But it was his normally vibrant complexion, now turned pasty and shrunken, that hit her hardest. Against the thick white hair, since the last time she saw Giovanni two months ago, the transformation was startling in the extreme.

'Are you going to stand there like a statue all day long?'

Allegra jumped at the gruff query. Her platform-heeled feet freed themselves from the shock and moved towards the figure, whose frailty was outlined harshly in the morning sun.

'Grandfather.' Allegra stopped, not sure of the appropriate words to tackle what was in front of her.

'Come. Sit down,' Giovanni Di Sione urged, patting the side of the bed with a gnarled hand.

She closed the gap and perched on the edge, swallowing a sob when her eyes met her grandfather's. She couldn't have borne it if the spirit of the indomitable man who'd arrived on Ellis Island over half a century ago had dimmed. But thankfully, his clear grey eyes were as piercing as ever, if a little shadowed with pain.

'Why didn't you tell me?' she whispered, her voice hoarse from the emotions she was trying to suppress. 'We've spoken on the phone so many times since I was last here. And why didn't you send for me sooner?'

'You had other things on your mind.'

Allegra frowned. 'Things like what?'

'I know how important the foundation gala was to you, and from the reports I've heard it was a rousing success. I didn't want you to worry about an old man when you had a big event needing your attention.'

'My work will never be as important to me as you are. You know that. You should've sent for me!'

A wry smile twisted his thin lips. 'Consider me suitably berated.'

Chagrined, Allegra shook her head. 'I'm sorry.'

'Don't be. Your quiet fire is one of the many things I'm proud of you for, *piccola mia*.' He held out a large hand and she placed hers in it. His touch was warm and reassuring, but her heart dipped to notice that it lacked its usual gripping strength. 'So, Matteo spoke to you?'

Swallowing hard, Allegra nodded. 'Your leukaemia is back? And the prognosis is a year if we're lucky?' Her voice shook with the question, and the pit in her stomach she'd been struggling to keep from widening yawned open as she stared back at her grandfather. With every fibre of her being she had wanted it not to be true, but heart in her throat, she watched Giovanni nod.

'*Sì,*' he confirmed, his eyes steady on hers in a way that told her he wouldn't let her shy away from the reality of the situation. 'And this time, there will be no medical intervention. The last time was risky enough, or so the doctors tell me.'

'There's absolutely *nothing* they can do? Are you sure? I could make some calls…'

'Allegra, *cara mia*, that is not why I asked you to come home. I have beaten the odds for over fifteen years since I was first diagnosed. I've had a good life, and been blessed in so many ways. I've accepted my fate. But before I go…'

'Please don't speak like that,' she pleaded.

Her grandfather regarded her with sympathy, then shook

his head. 'You will accept this, much as you've accepted so many hard things in your life. You are strong, Allegra *mia*. You will be even stronger for this challenge. I know it.'

Allegra wanted to childishly shut her ears, to dismiss the old man's philosophical waxing. But she'd never been one to bury her head in the sand. She'd been ejected from childhood to a role of responsibility over her younger siblings almost overnight. Alessandro, her oldest brother, and Dante and Dario, the twin hellions who'd made the life of every single person they came into contact with at the Di Sione mansion a misery, had been sent to boarding school as soon as they were old enough, but her three younger siblings had been *her* responsibility. And while she knew deep in her heart that she hadn't succeeded in her efforts to be the best role model for her sisters and brothers, she'd tried her damnedest to make their orphaned lives as easy as possible. In a world where nannies had come and gone with the frequency of a revolving door, and a grandfather who'd been fully immersed in building his empire, Allegra had tried to bring stability to her younger charges.

More often than not, she'd failed, and Giovanni had had to step in. While with each failure, she'd doubted her ability to be what she needed for her family, she'd never shied away from doing the right thing.

And the right thing was her family. Grandfather and her siblings came first and foremost. Always.

Stemming the pain slashing her heart, she took a deep breath and nodded. 'What do you need me to do?'

Whether it was the briskness in her voice or the hard acceptance that she couldn't change the wiles of fate that did it, her grandfather sat upright, his face showing a trace more colour than it had a few minutes ago. Allegra was grateful for it, even as her heart hammered at whatever he was about to ask of her. Giovanni wouldn't have summoned her if it weren't important.

'I need you to recover something for me. Something rare and precious that I lost a long time ago.'

Allegra nodded. 'Okay, I'll call the head of the investigative firm I use…'

'No, you misunderstand. I don't want this item found. I need it *recovered*. I already know where it is.'

She frowned. 'If you know where it is, then why don't you just send for it?'

Giovanni relaxed in his bed with a slight shake of his head. 'I need you to go and get it.'

'I don't understand.'

Her grandfather exhaled. 'Perhaps I need to elaborate. You remember the story of my Lost Mistresses?'

Warily, she nodded. 'The collection you told us about when we were kids? Matteo said you asked him to find one of them for you. So it's really true? They exist?'

A sad smile flitted over the old man's lips. 'Yes, my dear, it's true. I sold them off to get the capital to start our family business. But now…' His gaze drifted off and Allegra's heart lurched at the bleakness she witnessed. 'Now, I need them back. I *must* have them back before I die!'

Unable to deny the man whose love—even when it was distant and buried beneath the huge responsibility of caring for his numerous grandchildren—had never dimmed, she nodded. 'I'll find it for you, whatever it is.'

Giovanni sighed deeply. His head lolled against the snow-white pillow, but his gaze never wavered from hers. 'I knew I could count on you. If my memory serves me right, my beloved box was sold to a sheikh decades ago. He wanted it for his bride and, at the time, he made me an offer I couldn't refuse.' He smiled, although it was tinged with an even deeper desolation. 'Besides, who was I to stand in the way of true love?'

'Do you remember his name? Where he was from?' Allegra pressed, partly because she wanted the facts as quickly as possible so she could pull her grandfather from the memories that were clearly causing him such great sadness. The grandfather she remembered had always been focused very much in the here and now, the future of his family business and the welfare of his grandchildren, his paramount concern. To see him dwelling on the past he so rarely talked about heightened the fear of impending loss.

'I don't recall his first name, but he was the Sheikh of Dar-Aman. When we met, he was about to marry the woman of his dreams. He wanted the box as part of his wedding gift to her. It was one of many he'd accumulated over the years.'

'Nonno,' she murmured the Italian term she hadn't used in a long time. 'I'll do all I can to get it back, but you have to bear in mind that this was a long time ago. The box may have been sold on.' The last thing she wanted to do was disappoint her grandfather, but she had to prime him in case she hit a dead end.

Giovanni shook his head. 'No. I tried to buy it back after the sheikh lost his wife. He refused to part with it. He swore that he would never give it up. I tried one more time a few years ago without success. But it's still in the Dar-Aman palace.'

The conviction with which he said it made Allegra suspect her grandfather had been keeping a close eye on his precious box. Which made her wonder why he hadn't made moves to reacquire it before now.

The Di Sione name alone could open the most hallowed doors, never mind the fortune that went with it.

'Will you find it for me, my dear?' The plea in his voice was hard to miss. And hard to take in that he'd yearned secretly for this box, which he'd let go in order to lay a foundation for his family.

'Of course I will.' Whether it was a long shot or not,

Allegra intended to do her utmost to locate the box. 'How did you come about it in the first place?'

Her grandfather coughed, the rough sound echoing around the sun-drenched terrace. Then he began to wheeze. Panicked, Allegra jumped to her feet. 'Grandfather?'

Giovanni pointed feebly at the oxygen canister. She reached for it and settled the mask over his face just as an orderly rushed through the French doors.

Matteo had mentioned that the doctors had agreed for Giovanni to come home only if he arranged to have private medical care on-site. Nevertheless, the appearance of the nurse hammered home the severity of her grandfather's condition. And the fact that things would only get worse.

'I'm sorry, Miss Di Sione. He needs to rest now.'

Allegra watched the rapid rise and fall of her grandfather's chest with stinging eyes. 'Grandfather…'

He reached up and pulled down the mask, much to the disapproval of the nurse. 'It's okay. These bouts are short and much worse than they look. There's life in this old dog yet.' The brief twinkle in his eye triggered her smile, but the fear gripping her heart remained. When he reached for her hand again, she stepped closer.

'Bring me back the box, Allegra *mia*. It needs to come home.'

Nodding, she leaned down and kissed his pale cheek. 'I'll find it. I promise. Rest now, please.'

His grip tightened on hers for a brief moment before he let go.

Allegra walked away with a head full of questions and a heart filled with tears. Plucking her phone from her dress pocket, she dialled Matteo's number, then exhaled in frustration when it went straight to voicemail. She contemplated contacting the rest of her siblings, but discarded the thought. Besides Matteo and Bianca, she hadn't spoken to the rest of her brothers or sisters for a couple of weeks.

They all knew about their grandfather's illness, and would make time to see Giovanni when they could, but they led busy lives. She couldn't burden them with the sadness weighing her down.

Besides, she needed to get on with keeping her promise to her grandfather. A promise she intended to keep, come what may.

CHAPTER TWO

'ALLEGRA, IT'S TEN O'CLOCK.'

Allegra highlighted another section of the document she was reading with her marker pen, then glanced up.

'What?' she enquired absently, her mind still tackling how best to encourage the powers that be in the tiny Asia Pacific country to ratify a few more women's rights laws. As she'd found with countries great and small, diplomacy went a long way, but never far enough. She made a mental note to speak to her brother Alessandro about directing a few business deals to the country to grease her efforts. Allegra had learned the hard way that the lines of communication opened up wider with a promise of tangible reward. She'd fought too hard to win further rights for women in the country to let anything stand in the way at the last hurdle.

'Sheikh Rahim Al-Hadi's personal secretary agreed to grant you a fifteen-minute window, remember?' Her assistant, Zara, glanced at her watch and smiled. 'You now have fourteen minutes.'

Allegra dropped the marker pen with a grimace.

Wondering what sort of man she would be dealing with after her visit with her grandfather, Allegra had spent a quick half hour researching the Kingdom of Dar-Aman and its current ruling sheikh. Her initial discoveries had been appalling and an affront to everything she stood for as a champion of women's rights.

But she had a task to perform. A promise to keep.

Her fingers flew over the numbers and she breathed out as the line connected. 'Allegra Di Sione for Sheikh Al-Hadi, please,' she said calmly, trying and failing to erase the images of the sheikh's very vivid and very public playboy lifestyle, the pictures of gold-threaded sheets, diamond-studded mirrors and treasures in every room in the royal palace that were superimposed on her mind.

That those exploits and excesses were enjoyed at the cost of his kingdom's subjects made her hand tighten on the phone as she was put on hold.

Sultry Arab music filled the brief silence, the sounds so surprisingly beautiful and poignant Allegra's breath caught. She relaxed against her high-backed leather chair, a reluctant smile curving her lips as the hypnotic music washed over her, momentarily eclipsing every worry blotting her horizon.

Closing her eyes, she let her mind drift, back to a time when romance books had been her secret pleasure, her selfish escape. In a flash she was transported to hot Arabian desert nights and tall figures in flowing white robes. To whispered promises in the dark and soulful brown eyes that promised forever.

'Hello?'

Allegra jerked upright, chagrined that she'd missed the first prompt.

'Um… Sheikh Al-Hadi, thank you for taking my call.'

'You can thank me by stating the purpose of this call, and giving it the proper attention it deserves,' he replied, the pitch of the deep, masculine voice powering down her spine.

His intonation, the way his voice caressed the vowels of the words he spoke, threw Allegra for a moment. A moment too long, if the harsh exhalation at the end of the line was anything to go by.

She hurried to speak. 'My name is Allegra Di Sione...'

'I'm very much aware of who you are. What I'm still waiting to find out is *why* you wished to speak to me.'

She bit her tongue against an acerbic response. As the head of her family's charity, she'd been well practiced in diplomacy, even when she least felt it.

Allegra reminded herself why she was doing this, and regrouped. 'I have a matter to discuss with you—one of the utmost importance—which I'd prefer not to do over the phone.'

'Since you and I have never met before, I assume this matter you wish to discuss concerns your Di Sione Foundation?'

Allegra frowned, a little aghast by her body's unwanted but deeply decadent reaction to his voice.

The notion that the answer she gave would determine the course of this conversation made her hesitate. The matter she wished to discuss was intensely personal. She had no intention of failing her task. But neither did she want her access blocked before she'd even started her quest to regain the treasured box for her grandfather by admitting that her visit would be personal. For one thing, with the previous sheikh dead, she wasn't even sure Sheikh Rahim Al-Hadi was still in possession of the box Giovanni spoke so fondly of.

She framed her words carefully. 'I'll be visiting you in my capacity as the head of my family's foundation, yes,' she prevaricated, fighting the urge to cross her fingers.

She didn't believe in luck. Or fate. Or destiny. Or she would be unbearably heartbroken that the cosmos had seen it fit to orphan seven small children, then given the only loving substitute parent she'd known a life-threatening condition.

Life was what it was.

She'd long ago accepted the fleeting happiness along

with the abiding pain that came with being a Di Sione. Once she reached Dar-Aman, she would explain the true purpose of her visit.

If she got there.

'I'm leaving the capital on Thursday morning. Perhaps you can arrange to see me when I return in a month's time.'

'What? No. I need to see you before you go away.' Presumably to Europe or the Caribbean. After all, he was rumoured to keep homes in Monaco, St-Tropez and the Maldives. When her response was met with even more silence, she continued. 'Our business won't take more than a few hours, half a day at the most.'

'Very well. My private jet is currently hangared at Teterboro Airport. It's returning in two days. I'll have my people arrange for you to be on it.'

Allegra's mouth twisted. 'That won't be necessary. I'm perfectly okay with taking a commercial flight.' She couldn't quite keep the censure from her tone.

'Shall I make my own inference from your tone or do you wish to tell me why the offer of my jet offends you?' he rasped icily.

'There's the very small matter of concern about my carbon footprint.' It was a position she felt strongly about, even though it earned her ridicule from her brothers, who made use of private jets when they pleased.

'Very well. I'll leave you to discover for yourself the many connecting flights you'll need to take to reach Dar-Aman from New York. You might also want to bear in mind that the half a day window might be reduced to mere minutes if you arrive late. If you change your mind about my offer, let my secretary know. Your time is up and I have other pressing matters to attend to. Goodbye, Miss Di Sione.'

'Wait!'

'Yes?'

She clicked on her diary and scrutinised it quickly. The earliest she could get to the Kingdom of Dar-Aman were she to leave tonight—which was impossible because she had a dinner appointment with a UN ambassador—would be the early hours of Thursday morning after three flight changes. She would be in no state to have a coherent conversation with the sheikh, never mind attempt to make him a fair offer for the Fabergé box. Her grandfather's request was too important to arrive in Dar-Aman tired and ill-prepared.

'I...I accept your offer.'

'Good choice, Miss Di Sione. I look forward to welcoming you to Dar-Aman.'

Sheikh Rahim Al-Hadi perused the in-depth report his aide, Harun, had put together for him. After a second read, he closed the file and sat back from the large, polished antique desk hewn from one of the oak trees said to have been planted by the first man to have set foot on Dar-Aman. That man had been his direct ancestor, the first Sheikh Al-Hadi.

The responsibility ingrained into that desk wasn't lost on Rahim. Each time he sat down he felt its oppressive weight. Each time he made a decision that drew a frown, or a protest from a council mired in the old ways, the weight of that frustrating responsibility pressed down harder on him.

He smiled wryly.

There had been a time when he'd gladly have tossed the desk onto the pyre and gleefully watched it burn in an all-night bonfire. Preferably surrounded by three dozen sycophants and an endless supply of willing females.

Unfolding his arms, he touched the left side of his chin, where a remnant of his old ways resided in the form of a scar earned while abseiling down a sheer cliff face on a stupid dare.

That adrenaline-fuelled, life-endangering roller-coaster living had come to an abrupt end with the death of his father six months ago.

Then he'd been forced to return home. Forced to face the path his life had taken…

Cutting that mental road trip short, he pressed the intercom.

'Harun, have the state guest rooms in the east wing prepared. And delay my trip for another three days.'

'But… Your Highness…are you sure?' the middle-aged man enquired.

Rahim suppressed a sigh. He was sick to the back teeth of his chief aide's second-guessing. If the man weren't a veritable mine of information on everything to do with Dar-Aman, Rahim would've fired him a long time ago.

Rahim hadn't needed palace spies to tell him that Harun didn't want him in Dar-Aman. Had the decision been left to Harun alone when the council had presented Rahim with the 'Rule or Abdicate' choice, Harun would've preferred Rahim abdicate, so Harun's own son, Rahim's distant cousin, could take the throne.

But despite being presented with a decision he hadn't been expecting until he was well into his fourth or fifth decade, Rahim had known he had only one choice. Dar-Aman was his home. His ancestors had fought and sacrificed to keep this their home. Rahim wasn't about to turn his back on it because of hurt feelings or the sentimentality of youth. If anything, his eyes had been opened to the fact that love and fairy tales existed in the minds of the weak and foolish.

He'd thrived without those ephemeral emotions and there was certainly no room for that in the future of Dar-Aman. Just as there was no room to cater to Harun's sense of entitlement. But for now, Rahim needed him. Because until he wrought the changes he desperately needed to bring to his kingdom, his hands were tied. In so many ways that he'd lost count. And with each knot he unravelled, it seemed several more sprang up elsewhere.

'I also want a banquet held on Friday night. Make sure all the necessary dignitaries and ministers and their wives are invited,' he added.

'Of course, it will be done as you wish' came the reluctant reply. 'Do you require anything else, Your Highness?'

'If I do, I will let you know.'

'Yes, Your Highness.'

He disconnected, and strode back to the window. The view that greeted him was the same. Verdant grass rolled for almost a quarter mile from the grounds of the royal palace, interspersed in several places by shining mosaic fountains, majestic in stature and elaborately pleasing in their water displays. Much like everywhere in the royal palace, each facet of the landscape had been created with pleasure in mind. Everything his father had done had been first and foremost to please the wife he'd loved above everything and everyone else. Therefore his late father had spared no expense in providing the palace to rival the most magical and luxurious fairy tales, in order to please his mother.

While she'd been alive, that love had flowed to him, and beyond, to the Dar-Aman people. His home and kingdom had been a charmed place indeed.

And then she'd died, taking his unborn brother with her, and turning Rahim's world to darkness.

Rahim gritted his teeth as long-suppressed wounds threatened to rip open. Those wounds had been straining against the bandages of time since his return to the palace, a place he'd sworn on his eighteenth birthday never to return to. That last, blazing row with his father remained seared in his memory, along with the stiletto-sharp words his father had thrown at him that day. It had shocked him then how quickly fond and happy memories could be replaced with pain and desolation. But no matter how much he'd wished it otherwise, his mother's death had changed everything, including, for a very long time, his life's path.

Even his people hadn't been spared. Dar-Aman had suffered greatly since the death of its queen.

Shock didn't begin to cover his emotions at what Rahim had returned home to six months ago. And he had only himself to blame. From the moment he'd left Dar-Aman fifteen years ago, he'd mentally and emotionally cut all ties with his homeland. The people he'd surrounded himself with might have known he was the heir to a sheikhdom, but they'd been warned in no uncertain terms never to speak about his homeland. The blackout when it came to everything Dar-Aman had been complete.

Now he stared at the kingdom spread beneath him with regret and sadness.

Beyond the fairy-tale palace lay miles and miles of construction work, evidence of a painful rebirth where there should've been proud growth. Dar-Aman's infrastructure had been left in the hands of a corrupt and greedy few who'd run the economy to the ground until his return had put an end to the chaos. The government that was once held up by the international community as forward-thinking had been perverted to the point where they were almost archaic.

His mind veered from the monumental task that lay before him, to the impending visit of Allegra Di Sione. Although Rahim had crossed paths with the Di Sione twin brothers during his 'party hard' phase in college and afterwards, he hadn't taken much note of the rest of the dynastic family. After college, Rahim had been too busy forging a life for himself that didn't involve Dar-Aman, even though at the back of his mind he'd known he'd have to assume the mantle of sheikh one day. He'd built a successful hedge fund company worth billions, while living life to the fullest in every sense.

And all the while, his home had been crumbling into decay and apathy. While he could channel his own personal fortune into restoring his kingdom to the respectable powerhouse it'd once been, he was aware of the more problematic issue of his personal image, his past exploits having raised more than a few eyebrows since his return.

The attention-seeking antics of his teenage years, before he'd parted ways with his father, could have been explained away as youthful hormones.

But Rahim knew his less than conservative lifestyle was the reason he'd met with so much resistance since his return to Dar-Aman.

Turning from the window, he returned to his desk.

Allegra Di Sione's visit to Dar-Aman couldn't have come at a more opportune time. Her foundation's work on rights-enhancing on behalf of women, especially in poverty-stricken countries, was just the launching ground Rahim needed for his people. And it wouldn't hurt to have his own image makeover in the process.

The Dar-Amanian people needed to believe he was invested in their future. They needed to believe he wasn't just a playboy flashing by to throw money at a problem before disappearing again. He could do nothing about the reams of media reports about his high-octane lifestyle in the past decade. What he *could* do was demonstrate that he was here for the long haul. Once their confidence in him was restored, he could lay the firm foundations for his kingdom's future.

And Allegra Di Sione was the key to that plan.

Allegra rose and stalked to the door of the plane the moment the seat belt lights flashed off. The anger roiling through her belly threatened to rise up and choke her. She was ashamed that part of it was directed at herself.

She'd boarded the royal Dar-Aman jet with every intention of hating every minute of the fourteen-hour flight. Instead she'd melted into the soft, luxury leather club chair, and after a brief resistance, graciously accepted the care and attention the staff had lavished on her. Plus the peace and quiet had been heaven to work in, the state-of-the-art technology keeping her linked with her office. She'd even grudgingly accepted why her brothers highly rated private jet travel. With the amount of international business they conducted, the ability to work or rest in transit without distractions would be a godsend.

Allegra had even gone as far as to silently praise Sheikh Rahim Al-Hadi when one member of his plane staff had let slip that the jet was also used to transport food aid in the Arab region as and when needed.

But *all* of that had been before she'd opened the glossy magazine Zara had included in her hurriedly put together 'Things to Know about Dar-Aman' dossier. The article had juxtaposed life on the streets as a common citizen against life as the ruler of the oil-rich kingdom.

The dichotomy had been staggering.

Shock had held her rigid as she'd leafed through glossy picture after glossy picture showing the sheer, almost nauseating wealth displayed in the royal palace. Compared to the neglected citizens and woefully inadequate infrastructure, Allegra had been deeply saddened and angered as she'd taken in the gold-leaf ceilings and Fabergé boxes dotted in careless abandon in guests' rooms. Even the pillars and arches that flowed from hallway to room were painted with gold. Reaching the end of the article, she'd been truly stunned at the estimated wealth of the palace and its yearly upkeep. Since Zara had also included the annual gross domestic product of Dar-Aman in the dossier, Allegra had a direct comparison at her fingertips. The result had made her fingers clench hard around the magazine till she'd heard a rip.

That rip echoed through her now as she stepped into the early-morning sunshine and onto the red carpet and spotted the convoy of black SUVs speeding towards the plane. In the middle of the gleaming vehicles, with miniature royal flags billowing from the bonnets, was a top-of-the-line Rolls Royce Phantom.

Since one of her brothers had been toying with purchasing one last Christmas, Allegra knew the cost of the luxury car. She swung her gaze from the gleaming white, gold-trimmed car, to the man in flowing white robes striding towards her.

Her breath caught as she watched him move. Despite the crisp robes covering him from neck to ankles, she couldn't mistake the natural grace in his walk, or the animal awareness that whipped through his lean frame. As he drew closer, her gaze rose to his face.

Disgruntlement morphed to something else. Something equally all-consuming, but a lot more dangerous, as her eyes met golden hazel ones. Surrounded by long, sooty lashes, the gaze was direct, piercing in a way that made her step falter and grind to a halt. Ashamedly dazed, she took in the high cheekbones, the square, chiselled jaw which sat beneath neatly trimmed designer stubble and the aristocratic nose that flared slightly as he conducted his own inspection of her.

She'd met enough heads of state to separate the natural born leaders from those who relied on their position to throw their weight about. The sheer magnetism of the man who she'd only ever seen in a two-dimensional picture in a magazine didn't need the trappings of wealth, or the majestic Dar-Aman royal-crested *keffiyeh* that rested effortlessly on his proud head, to show he was an alpha in every sense of the word.

Allegra was still wrestling with the direction of her thoughts and the confusing emotions warring within her when he bared his teeth in a smile so charming and disarming her heart flipped in her chest.

'Miss Di Sione, it's good to meet you. Welcome to Dar-Aman. I'm Sheikh Rahim Al-Hadi. I would've been here to meet you earlier, but matters of the palace delayed my arrival. Please forgive me.'

Forcing her mouth not to gape at the raw sensuality and beauty of the man before her, Allegra scrambled to remember why she was incensed with this man and everything he stood for.

But he was holding out his hand, and being too polite and conscious she was greeting the ruler of a kingdom in full view of his members of state, she had no choice but to place her hand in his.

Fire sizzled up her arm. There was no other way to describe it. Allegra tore her gaze away and glanced down at where their hands joined to verify that he wasn't doing something absurdly juvenile, like zapping her with a hand buzzer. She knew it was possible because Dante, the crazier half of her twin set of brothers, had played that trick on her once.

There was no trick this time. Her fingers shook within his large, firm hold, the result sending goose pimples all over her body.

'That's quite all right. The last thing I expect is special treatment,' she added, once she'd clawed back a bit of sense.

After one further press of her flesh, he dropped her hand. Allegra wasn't sure whether to sigh with relief or rub her hand on her thigh to alleviate the tingle that lingered.

'You are an invited guest to Dar-Aman—that means

you're entitled to special treatment. Come and meet my council, then we will travel to the palace.' He stepped back and she noticed the small group that had surrounded them. A middle-aged man was the first to step forward. The disapproving gleam in his eyes took her aback for a moment.

'This is Harun Saddiq, my personal aide and advisor.'

Allegra summoned a smile. 'I believe we spoke on the phone. Thank you for your help in getting me here.'

The older man inclined his head and shook her hand, but offered no response. Allegra silently shrugged him off. Whatever issue he had with her, she wouldn't be here long enough for it to matter. She conducted the rest of the meet and greet with accustomed diplomacy, but as she turned away, she caught Sheikh Rahim's sharp gaze on her as he led her towards the luxury car.

The driver leapt forward, but Rahim Al-Hadi waved him away. Mildly surprised by the dismissal of protocol, Allegra glanced up. And met keen hazel eyes regarding her.

'Are you all right?' he asked.

The sensation was absurd, but she couldn't dismiss the idea that he was seeing more than she wanted him to. That he knew his effect on her. 'Yes, of course. Why shouldn't I be?'

One sleek eyebrow went up. 'It's perfectly acceptable to be exhausted and perhaps a little cranky after such a long flight.'

'I'm not cranky.' She paused, willing the snap out of her voice and reminding herself that she was here for her grandfather and nothing else. 'And you didn't need to come out and meet me. I would've been fine making my own way.'

'Perhaps I have ulterior motives for your visit.' He smiled, displaying perfect teeth in a sexy, dangerously arresting face that had her senses going into free fall.

Tucking her briefcase closer against her body, she dragged her gaze away, silently thankful for the reminder of Sheikh Rahim's playboy reputation. He was probably a man who saw every woman as a potential conquest.

'It's a shame I won't be here long enough to find out what they are,' she said, faking a smile as she slid into the back seat.

The door shut with a soft, decadent *whoosh*, and she watched, almost against her will, as he walked around to the opposite side from which he'd emerged to slide in next to her.

Outside, in the arid desert air, Allegra had only been visually aware of Rahim Al-Hadi's presence. Tucked in close proximity to him, his scent washed over her. Spicy, exotic, with a touch of sandalwood, the scent was powerful and overwhelmingly male.

She'd dated during her college years and afterwards, although none of her relationships had gone beyond the casual phase. She'd even indulged in a brief physical relationship when she'd been curious to see what she was missing that wasn't fulfilled by her work.

None of the men who'd crossed her path had had the effect that Rahim Al-Hadi had on her now. She surreptitiously drew in another breath and again sensations bombarded her.

Reassuring herself that she was blowing things out of proportion, probably due to lack of sleep, she cleared her throat. 'Your Highness, I'm grateful to you for agreeing to see me on such short notice. I promise I won't take up too much of your time.'

He sent her a wider, even more devastating smile, and in that moment Allegra knew her emotionally dazed state had nothing to do with lack of sleep. The man was sexual charisma personified. While the men she'd dated had had charm going for them, what this man wielded in his small finger alone would flatten them. She stared as his even white teeth gleamed in the brilliant sunshine. 'You'll be pleased to know I've rearranged my schedule to accommodate your visit. For as long as you're here, my staff and I are at your service. Any luxury you wish for will be yours with just the asking.'

And with that, Allegra was brought back to earth with a hard bump. The reminder of Rahim Al-Hadi's unspeakable wealth made her bristle. 'Thank you, but the luxury of my hotel bed and a cup of strong coffee are all I'll need once I've discussed the reason for my visit with you. My return flight is booked for tomorrow, so I hope you won't think me rude if I insist on our meeting as soon as possible?'

Straight black brows clamped together in a thunderous frown. 'You're leaving tomorrow?' he rasped, the gleam of his teeth disappearing as his full, sensual lips compressed in a displeased line.

'You did mention you would only be available for a short time, did you not, Your Highness?'

'Rahim.'

'Excuse me?'

'You may call me Rahim when we are having a one-to-one conversation,' he elaborated, but his smile this time lacked its previous warmth. It was almost as if she'd done something to offend him. 'May I call you Allegra?'

For a moment, she lost herself to the sensual intonation of her name. While his accent was mostly American—due to his having spent over a decade and a half in the US—every now and then the exotic tones of his homeland's dialect curled around his words, lending them a mesmeric quality.

'I... Yes, of course.' In a distant part of her mind, Allegra knew she should be thankful that this meeting was going better than she'd hoped it would.

'Allegra, I confess to not giving our telephone conversation the careful attention it deserved.' Another blinding smile that slammed lightning straight to her midriff. 'After we spoke I had a change of heart. I've already prepared rooms in my palace for your convenience. My trip has also been postponed to Sunday, which means I will devote myself to you until then. Tonight, I'm holding a banquet in your honour.'

Her mouth gaped. 'A *banquet*? But I'm only here to discuss…'

He waved her protest away with a flick of an elegant hand. 'We'll discuss your business here later, after you've had a chance to rest. For now, allow me to give you a brief tour of Shar-el-Aman, my country's beautiful capital.'

Allegra swallowed her surprise, although the notion that there was more going on here than met the eye didn't dissipate.

'I really wasn't expecting you to go to all this trouble,' she started.

'But you will humour me nonetheless, yes?'

Unable to think of a way to dissuade him, she nodded. 'If you wish.'

'I wish.'

The satisfied smile her response produced drew her attention to his mouth. As male specimens went, Rahim Al-Hadi had inherited more than his fair share of good looks. It was no wonder he'd been voted the world's most eligible bachelor more times than Allegra cared to count. It was probably also why he thought that smile could win any man, woman or child round to his way of thinking.

It's won you over, hasn't it?

She suppressed the irritating observation and followed his finger as he pointed out a sprawling group of buildings nestled on a hilltop. 'That's our state university. Dar-Aman University boasts world-class academics and state-of-the-art facilities.'

Within ten minutes he'd drawn her attention to several more of Dar-Aman's highly regarded treasures. When he pointed out yet another monument, whose sole purpose was to provide superficial pleasure, she couldn't hold her tongue.

'Fountains and memorials with gold-plated plaques are all very nice to look at, I'm sure, but Dar-Aman's current economic situation is a little bit more pressing, don't you think?' Allegra's earlier anger began to resurface.

The arm he'd raised to indicate yet another statue dropped a fraction. 'My mother loved beautiful things. And my father couldn't say no to granting them to her. As to my country's economic situation, I have it well in hand, Allegra.'

'Do you? Not according to world views,' she replied before she could curb her response.

He stiffened, his eyes narrowing as his gaze zeroed in on her. 'And do you believe everything you read in the papers?' His voice had turned arctic.

Allegra cleared her throat, the knowledge that the information in the report she'd read on the plane had been hastily put together by her assistant suddenly flaring in her mind and giving her pause. 'I didn't mean to cause offence.'

'On the contrary, I think you meant to make an exact point. Perhaps you want to elaborate on what you mean?'

They stared at one another for a charged moment, the tense atmosphere burning between them. Allegra shook her head to clear it, and also to backtrack a little before things got out of hand.

'I didn't mean to put it quite that way. Trust me, I'm a lot more diplomatic than that usually, or I'd be out of a job by now.' She gave a little laugh in the hope of alleviating the tension, but his continued stony regard tightened her skin. Almost afraid to breathe in case she'd done irreparable damage to her chances of retrieving her grandfather's treasure, she continued hurriedly. 'I simply meant I know that not everything is shiny and rosy in the Kingdom of Dar-Aman so this tour really isn't necessary.'

His mouth tightened. 'Look around you, Allegra. My country is in the middle of a rebirth, yes, but things are far from dire. The tour wasn't intended to pull the wool over your eyes. I was merely extending the hospitality that is afforded any invited guest. Unless things have changed in the States since I lived there, your president doesn't parade his state guests through the ghettos on the way to the White House, does he? In all things he puts his best foot forward, does he not?'

Feeling chastised, Allegra nevertheless cursed the heat washing into her face. 'No, he doesn't, but I can't help but mourn what was once a unique and powerful kingdom...' Her voice drifted off when she realised she was letting her personal feelings cloud what should be a clinical transaction. What Rahim Al-Hadi chose to do with his wealth and about his people's suffering wasn't part of her visit. 'I just didn't want you to waste your time with all this... schmoozing.' She bit her lip when his eyebrows elevated and a mildly censorious look crossed his face. Then his face turned thoughtful before he nodded. Pressing an intercom next to his elbow, he spoke rapidly in Arabic.

'We will head to the palace now. When you're better rested, I hope you'll be more receptive to what my kingdom has to offer.'

She frowned. 'I'm not sure I know what you mean.'

'It's clear you have preconceived notions where my kingdom and I are concerned.'

'Do you blame me?'

His jaw tightened briefly before he exhaled. 'No. And while it's understandable, I assure you that some situations—as well as individuals—are not irredeemable if things are handled expertly.'

'I think that depends on who does the handling, don't you?'

To her surprise he nodded readily. 'Indeed it does. And I prefer to think of this period as the darkness before the light shines once more on my people.'

She firmed her lips. 'True change comes not with words but with actions.'

'Then I look forward to showing you what I mean.'

He'd once again become the charming host whose smile upset the regular rhythm of her heartbeat, but Allegra didn't miss the shrewd and assessing gleam in his eyes each time he looked at her, or miss the fact that his gaze lingered on her face, and brushed down her body a few more times than her flailing senses could deal with.

By the time their convoy rolled through wide pillared gates manned by armed soldiers, Allegra understood why women fell over themselves to be his playthings. Rahim Al-Hadi wielded his voice, his body and his keen intelligence the way a composer wielded his baton.

Had she not vowed a long time ago never to get involved in relationships, especially volatile ones like the one that had ultimately seen her parents dead at a young age, Allegra was sure she'd have been swayed by Rahim's magnetic charm.

But she'd been immune to the charms of men for a long time, ever since she'd recognised that she didn't have what it took to make a man happy or to build a loving home. Even after watching her mother fail ceaselessly to change her father and to make a home in which her children were secure and safe, Allegra had believed she could take a different path, succeed where her mother had failed. Seeing her every effort turn to dust, and her sisters and brothers grow apart, had spelled her own spectacular failure in her ability to create a home or make another human happy.

Divesting herself of emotional entanglements after her one attempt at a relationship had failed had almost been a relief. It had freed her to pursue a cause she excelled in.

Her work was her life. She was safe from lethally charming, emotional landmines like Rahim Al-Hadi.

Suitably rearmoured, Allegra turned her attention to her surroundings. They were driving down a dual carriageway, the palm-lined road made of white stone. To the left and right, the blue waters of the Arabian Sea sparkled like a million tiny jewels in the distance. Before them, set atop a sprawling hill, the royal palace sat, a white, elaborate, triple gold-domed structure that could've been reproduced straight from an Arabian fairy tale.

Even from the outside, she knew the magazine pictures hadn't done the palace justice. And despite reminding herself what the cost of this palace meant to the rest of the Dar-Amanian people, Allegra found herself leaning forward, absorbing the breathtaking structure as the Rolls Royce slowed and stopped.

'My God. It's stunning!'

'Yes. It's the jewel in the crown that is my beloved homeland. I hope you will make it your home too, for a short while.'

CHAPTER THREE

RAHIM WATCHED HER eyes widen at his words, and wondered if he'd overplayed his hand. He was still irritated by her veiled comments about his leadership and the general state of Dar-Aman. As much as he'd wanted the disapproving Miss Di Sione delivered to the airport and sent on the next plane back to the US, he'd curbed his tongue, and laid on the charm.

'Thank you,' she murmured in response to his offer of hospitality.

'I looked further into your foundation's work and must commend you for the extraordinary results you've achieved in so short a time.' Everything he'd learned so far had solidified the belief that she was the one who could turn things around for him.

What he hadn't counted on was her sharp tongue. Or her beauty.

Despite willing himself not to do so, he found his gaze drawn back to her as a light blush rose up her neck. Her rich, chocolate hair was pulled back a little too severely and knotted with a clip at her nape for him to know whether the tresses were the sexy waves he preferred or straight. And her flawless skin had a golden hue to it, as if she'd recently spent time in a hot climate.

'My team and I are committed to what we do, but the people we work with do most of the work. I find that if the people I try to help *want* that change it happens quicker and lasts much longer than if they're spouting rhetoric simply to garner whatever political clout they need to attain immediate power.' Her words flowed with an innate passion that caught and held his attention. Her mouth, painted a neutral colour, was naturally full and plump, with a mole above her upper lip that drew his attention every time she spoke.

'You're passionate about your work.'

'I am. I take what I do very seriously.'

'As do I, Allegra.'

Deep azure eyes met his. Despite their heavy scepticism, the colour reminded him of the whirlpools he used to play in as a child at his family's beach house outside the city.

From nowhere his mother's voice cautioning him to be careful lest he got sucked into the water flared across his mind. The memory was vivid and unexpected, enough to make him frown.

Shrugging away the mildly unsettling feeling as an inevitable consequence of the decisions he knew he had to make concerning his kingdom, he looked at Allegra, and found her staring back at him.

'Is something wrong? I really don't mind staying at the hotel if…'

'I'm a man of my word, Allegra. I extended an invitation. I will not take it back.'

Alighting, he extended his hand to help her out. He saw her hesitate a moment before accepting his aid. A whisper of a smile touched his lips.

He'd also experienced the sizzle when they'd touched back at the airstrip. Back then he'd thought it a figment of his imagination. Or a product of his year-long abstinence. Sex had been the last thing on his mind once he'd found out his father had fallen ill and died without Rahim's knowledge. Guilt and bitterness had effectively killed his libido, and he'd been in no hurry to resurrect it once he'd arrived in Dar-Aman and seen what his father's apathy and neglect had caused his people. What the result of his own disinterest and self-imposed estrangement had wrought.

Allegra's hand slid into his. Heat flared in his belly and arrowed straight to his groin. Beneath the flowing robes of his *abaya*, his heart thundered as he stared down into her eyes, then to the colour surging beneath her silky skin.

He had no intention of bedding Allegra Di Sione, but he'd bedded enough women to know his effect on them. Sexual tension was a hugely effective tool. One he would shamelessly use to get Allegra to do his bidding if that was what it took.

Holding on to her hand, he let his thumb caress the soft space between her fingers. She gave a tiny gasp and tried to pull her hand away.

Rahim held on, absently aware that he was getting just as equally affected by the attraction crackling between them. But he had enough control not to allow it to go too far. He would play on it only until he got what he needed from her. He blithely ignored the sting of his conscience.

'Welcome to my palace,' he murmured.

She blinked, then jerked and looked around her before glancing back at him. 'I... Thank you.'

With one last caress, he allowed her hand to drop, aware that Harun and a few advisors lingered close by.

He strolled through the quadruple doors that led into the extensive space too large to be named a hallway. Two dozen pillars, which had provided endless amusement to play hide-and-seek as a child, rose from the floor and flared in gold and silver painted tentacles to the ceiling.

Beneath his feet, gold and silver inlaid marble floors gleamed and echoed his and Allegra's footsteps as they crossed the wide expanse to the east wing.

Rahim was aware of Allegra's suppressed gasps with each new visually stunning Moorish archway and new room they passed through. For the first time in his life, he was forced to see his home through another's eyes. Objets d'art and rare, priceless paintings he'd taken for granted since birth took on a new meaning. The precious collectibles his father had showered on his mother were laid out in cabinets and displayed on shelves and walls at every turn.

A touch of unease fizzed through him at the thought of the excessive display of wealth—which, now that he took a moment to acknowledge, bordered on the obscene—and he gave a small sigh of relief when they walked through another archway and reached the double doors he sought.

Allegra glanced behind her. 'We're alone,' she observed. Then she blushed, hurrying to elaborate. 'I mean, I thought your advisors were accompanying us so they could speak to you.'

'They are, but they're not allowed in the women's wing. Only I am.'

Her lips pursed in an unmistakable show of anger. Her eyes flashed before she lowered them. 'The *women's* wing? And you have the access-all-areas pass because you're the sheikh, I suppose?'

'Naturally.'

'And here I thought you were a modern man, Your Highness. You do realise that some would think you positively archaic that you still segregate your women?'

'I've never been one for popularity contests. And there is a good reason for keeping separate sleeping quarters for the women under my roof.'

Her mouth worked, as if she wanted to challenge him as to what those reasons were. Before she could, the doors to the suite were thrown open.

The young girl who emerged took one look at him and dropped to her knees with a loud gasp.

'Your Highness, everything is ready as you requested.'

'Good. You may stand up now, Nura.'

She scrambled up, but kept her head bent low.

He turned to Allegra. 'Nura will be your personal maid while you're here. If you need anything...'

'It really is unnecessary. I don't need a maid.' Allegra sent a stiff smile the young girl's way. At Nura's crestfallen expression, she added, 'I'm sorry, but I'm used to taking care of myself, and I don't want to waste your time. Time I'm sure will be better spent elsewhere?'

Irritation bubbled beneath Rahim's effort to remain a civil host. 'Nura will remain here. Every member of the palace staff has a role. Nura's is serving you during your stay.' When Allegra continued to look mutinous, he exhaled in frustration. 'Things are done a little differently here, Allegra. The earlier you accept that, the smoother your visit will be. I'm sure we both want that?'

'We do,' she replied tersely.

'Good. Then it's settled.'

Her gaze clashed and battled with his, but she didn't respond. Instead she followed Nura into the suite, the young maid's eagerness garnering a less stiff smile from Allegra.

He followed, despite the pressing awareness that he was needed elsewhere. While she was absorbed in the room that his own mother had used as a girl before marrying his father and relocating to the royal bedchamber, Rahim's gaze traced her elegant neck, lower to her slender waist and rounded bottom, to the slit at the back of Allegra's dress, which displayed her elegant legs.

Again heat stamped through him, harder this time, reminding him that he was very much a red-blooded male, who'd gone too long without the release that had been his to take once upon a time.

He'd taken and indulged a little too much in hindsight.

A predicament he wouldn't be able to fix without Allegra's help. The reminder curbed the insane need to reach out and trace his hand over that trim waist, change that expression on her face from condemnation to something more…malleable.

Halting the direction of his thoughts, he refocused his attention higher. She held one of the many trinket boxes that had been his mother's personal joy, her interest keen as she examined it.

Sensing his regard, she hastily placed the Russian artefact down and faced him.

'When will we have a chance to talk, Your Highness?' she asked.

'I have back-to-back meetings this morning, and engagements outside the palace this afternoon. We will speak after the banquet.' It would give him time to summon a few key people he trusted to meet her tonight. Rahim was confident once he laid out his immediate and long-term plans for Dar-Aman, she would revise her preconceived views.

'Oh. I'd hoped we could speak sooner.'

Rahim shook his head. 'My meetings this afternoon are outside the city. The tribal lands aren't exactly a hospitable place for…'

'A woman?' she inserted, her chin raised in challenge.

'For *anyone* not used to a harsher climate. Besides the rough terrain, I'll be travelling when the sun's at its peak. Heatstroke is a credible threat, one I would be remiss not to point out.'

'Oh…well, it won't be a problem for me. I came prepared.' She left the display cabinet and moved closer. In her heels, she came up to his chin. Her eyes met his, bold and clear. 'I could come with you. We would make efficient use of the time and talk on the way?' Her head tilted and the subtle scent of her perfume hit his nostrils.

Rahim breathed her in, struggling momentarily with the desire to lean in closer, place his mouth at that juncture between neck and shoulder where her pulse throbbed. Dragging his gaze from that tempting area, he looked down at her.

'Are you always this impatient, Allegra, or just *efficient* to the point of risking your health?' he murmured.

Harun had voiced his suspicion that her visit might be a secret scouting mission, to see if Dar-Aman fitted the criteria for the Di Sione Foundation's charity work. Rahim had dismissed the idea, but now he wondered whether his aide was right. She had made her opinion clear of what she thought of his kingdom.

'I'm just not one to sit around twiddling her thumbs. I'm here, and I'm not as frail or susceptible to the harshness of the desert as you think, so if it's not too much trouble, I'd like to come with you.' The determination in her voice spoke of a will that intrigued him. Not to mention his inability to look away from her alluring face. 'Please, Your Highness. This is important to me.'

Her soft plea echoed the softer look in her eyes. Had he not witnessed her displeasure before, Rahim would've been fooled into thinking she was trying to seduce him.

But his instincts warned him that despite the vivid, unmistakable attraction that whipped between them, Allegra Di Sione, the head of the Di Sione Foundation, was here for one reason only—to vet his kingdom.

Releasing an inner smile, Rahim nodded. He would play along. He had no intention of granting her a meeting until *he* was sure he'd satisfied every criteria her foundation needed to work with him. 'Very well. Provided you're rested and ready to go at three, you may accompany me.'

Her smile hit him off guard, its dazzling brilliance striking the heart of his awakening libido. As he stepped back and prepared to walk away, he experienced a tinge of regret that the possibility of Allegra Di Sione in his bed would never materialise.

'Thank you, Rahim.'

His brisk nod didn't dissipate the effect of hearing his name said seductively in that polished New York accent. In fact, he heard its sultry echoes long after he sat down to his first meeting of the morning.

Soft, insistent beeps from her phone's alarm woke Allegra three hours later, giving her ample time to get ready so Rahim wouldn't have any excuse to leave her behind.

She didn't need a crystal ball to guess that his reluctance stemmed from the need to hide the true extent of Dar-Aman's deterioration from her. Although why that would bother him now, when he'd failed to do much in the years as crown prince and in the six months since he took the throne, was beyond her. It was true that his kingdom was undergoing a resurgence economically, but the change was new and shaky, and in Allegra's view, far too late in coming.

Disappointment flared through her, but she curbed it and focused on her goal.

She might not have achieved the quick meeting, followed by a swift departure after they'd agreed terms for Rahim to sell her back her grandfather's long-lost box, but she was still on point. With any luck, she'd be back in New York within twenty-four hours.

Tilting her head back on the pillow, she sighed and allowed herself a brief, awed absorption of her surroundings.

The headboard above her head was beyond anything she'd ever seen before. Made up of richly embroidered panels in red and ochres connected together with gold thread, it rose halfway to the ceiling. Resting on a raised dais, the bed itself boasted expensive satin sheets and a heavy coverlet in colours that complemented the rest of the room.

Allegra had grown up with enough wealth for her not to be reverential over most luxuries, and yet each new discovery in the Dar-Aman palace took her breath away.

Her gaze lowered and swung across the room to the exquisitely carved console table, on which rested six stunning pieces of art. The intricately designed eggs were immediately recognisable as the much-fabled Fabergé eggs once belonging to the Russian dynasty. And those weren't the only jaw-dropping items in the room.

Everywhere Allegra looked, objects of priceless beauty graced surfaces, from rare Egyptian coins in glass cabinets to solid gold bridal head ornaments from India.

The article she'd read on the plane had mentioned Rahim and his parents as being great collectors of art. But how could they find beauty in inanimate objects while the economy suffered?

A knock came on the door before she could let loose the frustration growling through her belly. At Allegra's beckon, Nura entered, her slippered feet gliding silently across the marble floor.

'Mistress, can I get you anything? Some tea and sandwiches, perhaps? Or I can summon your personal chef to prepare a light meal if you wish?'

'No, Earl Grey tea with a dash of lemon and sandwiches would be perfect, thank you.'

Nura lifted a nearby phone and relayed the request, then turned just as Allegra was making her way to the bathroom.

'You are travelling outside the city walls with His Highness this afternoon?' she enquired. At Allegra's nod, she continued. 'You're going to visit the Nur-Aram tribe. It is the place I was named after.' She smiled, then worry creased her youthful face. 'It is a difficult place to get to. The journey can be quite rough.'

'It's fine,' Allegra reassured. 'I've visited worse places, I'm sure.'

Nura continued to look worried, but then dashed forward when Allegra reached the wide marble bathtub. 'I will draw your bath for you, Mistress.'

'Please, call me Allegra.'

Nura looked horrified, her soft brown eyes widening in alarm. 'No, I cannot.'

Surprised, Allegra asked, 'Why not?'

'Because it would be disrespectful to call a mistress of His Highness by her first name.'

Allegra wasn't sure why her stomach dropped and rolled with such acrobatic skill it would've made an elite athlete proud. She was pretty sure something had been lost in translation. Or assumptions had been made because of where Rahim had placed her in his palace? 'Are there a lot of mistresses in this wing?' she blurted before she could stop herself.

Nura nodded. 'At this time of the year, all of the fifteen residences are occupied.'

Nausea rose in Allegra's belly. She tried to bite her tongue, but the next question spilled out anyway. 'And all the fifteen occupants…they're related to Sheikh Rahim?'

Nura looked puzzled as she straightened from checking the temperature of the four gold-plated taps that gushed water into the cavernous bath. 'No, they are not His Highness's relations. But they're very important to him.'

Allegra tried to laugh but the sound came out skewed. 'Wow, next you'll be telling me there's a secret passage between this wing and the sheikh's bedchamber, like in the movies.'

Nura's laugh was more natural, a shy twinkle in her eye as she plucked warming towels from a rail and laid them within arm's reach of the bath. 'There is a connecting passage, but it's not *secret*. Everyone knows it is the last door along this hallway.'

Allegra's nausea increased. She'd visited enough cultures around the world on behalf of her charity to know that harems and the taking of concubines were still a *thing*, even in the twenty-first century.

She didn't know how else to ask the question burning on her tongue without coming straight out with it—*does the sheikh keep concubines?*—so she pulled hard on her diplomatic nerve and bit back the urge.

As detestable as the idea was, it was none of her business. Rahim Al-Hadi's sexual conquests, singular or numerous, shouldn't be something she wasted valuable time or brain matter over.

With a wrench at the master tap, she shut the water off. 'Thanks for your help, Nura. I've got it from here.'

The young woman vacillated for a second, then nodded enthusiastically. 'I'll go and lay out your clothes and toiletries.'

Allegra smothered a groan, kept the smile pinned in place until the elaborately carved wooden doors shut behind her. Sliding into the richly scented bath, she reined in her rioting feelings.

Sure, the sizzling heat that passed between them when they touched and the shock waves of sensation that blanketed her each time their eyes met were undeniable.

But there was no way she was about to forget that the man whose palace she was currently a guest in was a notorious playboy, whose exploits were vividly documented.

Rahim Al-Hadi treated women like they were playthings to be used and discarded the moment the shine wore off.

He'd placed her in the *women's wing where he kept his harem*, for heaven's sake. And by doing so, he'd proven conclusively that he was—contrary to his statement in the car—completely irredeemable.

CHAPTER FOUR

'YOU READY TO hit the road?' a deep voice said from behind where she stood examining a Gerhard Richter painting.

Allegra turned and swallowed a breath of surprise. Added to Rahim's much more informal tone, he'd shed his ceremonial office clothes for a black cotton *abaya*, with similar coloured *keffiyeh* and white *iqal*. But the combination was somehow more potent. Perhaps it was because the lighter material emphasised the breadth of his shoulders and skimmed his lean hips and thighs.

Or she was going out of her mind ogling a man she had zero interest in. She drew her gaze from his well-formed chest and redirected her eyes to his face, taking care to pin a neutral smile to hers.

Sure, with his informal clothes and his easy smile, Allegra could've fooled herself into thinking she was about to step out for coffee with a regular Joe.

But he wasn't. Rahim was a Dar-Amanian sheikh with a royal bloodline tracing back dozens of generations, and the wealth to match.

A wealth he hadn't seen fit to share with his people.

'Yes,' she responded, a little terser than she'd intended.

He shot her an assessing look but said nothing as he gestured for her to precede him out of the reception room where she'd been ushered to await his arrival.

Staunchly vowing to keep her emotions and opinions in check, she cleared her throat as they once again travelled through endless magnificently decorated reception rooms and hallways. 'How did your meetings go?'

'Are you really interested?'

She saw the mocking light in his eyes and chose to ignore it. 'Of course. I wouldn't ask if I wasn't.'

'The first one went as expected. The two that followed went badly,' he replied.

'You don't seem too cut up about it.'

He shrugged. 'Because I was prepared for it. I expected them to go badly. I would've been more surprised if they'd progressed smoothly.'

'Why?'

'Then I'd have known I was being lied to, and the meeting would've taken a turn for the very unfortunate.' The smile hardened, a dangerous light entering his eyes.

'Why?' she parroted one more time.

'Because I hate subterfuge in every form. I prefer my opponents to be straight up with me, even if the outcome of our confrontation is potentially disadvantageous to me.'

The thinly veiled warning lanced a spear of ice down her spine. She hadn't done anything wrong. She just hadn't had time to fully apprise Rahim Al-Hadi of her reason for visiting his kingdom. But still guilt flared high, because after her bath, while Nura had been busy fetching her tea, Allegra had conducted a thorough search of her rooms to see if by a stroke of luck the box was present. She had no intention of leaving without the box, but the right thing to do was to speak to Rahim as originally planned, not go behind his back searching for it herself.

'Of course,' she murmured when it became clear he was expecting a response.

With a tiny compression of his lips, he nodded. 'Good. Come this way. Our ride awaits.'

He led her through a wide golden arch straight out of

an *Arabian Nights* tale. Allegra had to content herself with gaping for a few seconds before they emerged into a wide courtyard the size of a football field. The edges were dotted with the ever-present fountains and several sitting areas, but at the end of it, set upon a large stone circle, were sleek helicopters, decorated with the royal colours and Dar-Amanian emblem.

'We're travelling by helicopter?' she asked as Rahim made a beeline for the aircraft, followed closely by two bodyguards.

'For most of the way, then we finish the journey by Jeep. Sure you still want to come?' His gaze seemed to intensify on her face as he said that.

Allegra summoned a smile, determined not to give Rahim an excuse to postpone their meeting. 'Of course.'

She pulled on the hat she carried, thankful that she always made a point of travelling prepared for every contingency, and double-checked that she had her phone tucked into her khaki cargo pants.

They reached the first large black aircraft. A guard held the door open. Before she could climb in Allegra found herself hoisted up by strong arms. Rahim's solid, overwhelming presence was a wall of heat at her back, shocking her into gasping when his groin connected to her backside for a searing second. The sensation was so alien she froze for a moment.

'You're not afraid of heights, are you?' he asked, his mouth so close to her ear his breath washed over her skin.

She suppressed a shiver. 'No, I'm not.'

His hand tightened on her arm for a second, before he deposited her in the front seat. Then he rounded the chopper to join her. 'Good, then you'll enjoy the experience. Fasten your seat belt,' he instructed after handing her a set of noise-cancelling headphones.

Allegra did as she was told. She tried not to watch his

sure hands as he readied the aircraft, but the elegant grace with which he handled the controls was astonishingly mesmerising. Dragging her gaze away, she saw other guards piling into the remaining choppers.

Her mouth twisted as Rahim pulled back the throttle and the chopper lifted away from the palace grounds. 'Do you always travel with such a large contingent of bodyguards?' she asked, glancing at the other two aircrafts that lifted off behind them.

'I've halved my bodyguards in the past three months. I can't reduce their number any further.'

'Why not?'

'Because that would be breaking protocol.'

She raised a cynical eyebrow. 'A protocol that insists you have almost two dozen bodyguards. Isn't that overkill?'

He shrugged. 'I'm good at taking care of myself.' A shadow clouded his eyes for a second before the hazel depths cleared again. 'I've been doing so for a long time. But laws are laws.'

'Laws can also be changed, especially if it's in the interest of your people, can they not?'

His gaze sharpened. 'Of course. But change doesn't happen overnight. Most often it's a long and arduous process.'

'Only if those who seek to unjustly benefit from it choose to stand in its way. It usually takes someone fearless enough who believes in doing the right thing for true change to happen.'

He nodded. 'I agree.'

'You do?'

He took his eyes off the controls to glance at her. 'You seem surprised, Allegra. Why wouldn't I agree with such a sound assessment?'

Allegra swallowed the automatic response that rose to

her lips. 'Not a lot of people welcome the views of women, especially when it comes to matters of state.'

'Then it's a blessing that I'm not one of them, is it not?' he said with a smile.

She stared at him, wondering if he was toying with her or cunning enough to think he would get away with voicing such barefaced lies. Especially after the speech he'd made about his dislike of subterfuge.

'Your Highness…'

'Rahim,' he invited softly.

Allegra glanced pointedly at the bodyguards seated behind them.

'It's fine. They cannot overhear us unless you raise your voice. Besides, I like the way you say my name,' he said softly.

She gasped, her face heating up as his gaze raked her body, then settled on her mouth. 'I don't think this is appropriate,' she blurted out before she could stop herself.

A sinfully wicked smile curved his lips. 'Then I'll spare your sensibilities and direct my conversation to more appropriate topics. Tell me about yourself.'

'Why?' she asked in surprise, all sense of diplomacy gone.

'I'm hoping it'll be a much better way to pass the time since other subjects trigger an almost…volatile reaction from you?'

She inhaled sharply at his acute reading of her emotions. Contrary to thinking she was making a decent pass at remaining neutral where Dar-Aman was concerned, Rahim had seen right through her.

And he wanted to change the subject. Her continued disappointment with a man she knew better than to hope was even remotely redeemable deepened. She shook her head. 'If you don't mind, I'd like to talk to you about the reason for my visit,' she pressed.

'I'd prefer to wait until I can give you my full, undivided attention. You deserve that. Until then, tell me how you came to start your foundation.'

Effectively stymied, she looked down at the desolate but indescribably beautiful landscape beneath her, momentarily dragged down memory lane.

The memories of her mother had grown hazy over the years, but a few precious conversations had remained vivid in her mind, popping up when she least expected them.

First and always, be your own person. Then your voice will be heard. Don't be like me, Allegra...

Anna Di Sione had delivered that particular out-of-the-blue warning as a six-year-old Allegra draped herself in her mother's pearls, content that this was a singular pleasure that she wouldn't have to compete with her siblings for. It had been one of the precious moments she'd spent with her mother that had been theirs alone.

'I took a gap year after high school, did the whole volunteering while touring the world thing. I suppose in a way I was finding myself.' She shrugged, uncomfortable about revealing an important part of what had forged her path in life. When she risked a glance at him, he returned her gaze with nothing but cordial interest. 'Anyway, I found out very quickly that some of the basic things I'd taken for granted were considered impossible luxuries or even forbidden to women in some countries. When I returned home, I discussed it with my grandfather. He started the foundation the year before I graduated from college and I took over and expanded it globally.'

Rahim nodded thoughtfully. 'Along with its reputation. You should be proud.'

Alarming warmth flowed through her at the compliment. 'I am. But it hasn't been easy. Sadly, as long as men think they're in charge, it'll be an uphill battle.'

His laugh sent a rumble of sensation down her body. His eyes gleamed with an intense light. 'You'll find that I'm not averse to a woman taking charge when the situation calls for it.'

'You don't find it an affront to your manhood?'

'My manhood is secure and robust enough to welcome the challenges of the fairer sex,' he drawled, his voice deep and mesmerising. 'I relish it, in fact. But that is not to say I don't assert control when it's needed.'

'Control? Over your women?'

Another smile. This one carnal and lethal. 'Are we straying into personal sexual territory, Allegra?'

Heat rose up her neck and stung her face, but she didn't glance away. 'Just verifying that we're talking about the same thing here.'

His smile disappeared and his eyes narrowed. 'What do you think I mean?'

She tried to shrug but the motion was too heavy. 'Physical force against women...'

'Is abhorrent to me and a crime in my kingdom,' he inserted thickly. 'One I fully endorse completely and utterly. Let there be no misunderstanding about that.'

The force behind his words caused her to swallow. 'I... Of course. To be honest, I'm not sure how this conversation took a left turn.'

He jaw flexed as he banked the chopper towards the west. 'Psych 101 would suggest a degree of Freudianism. Would I be right?'

Alarm sparked through her at how close he was skating to truths she didn't want to uncover. 'You haven't known me long enough to make that inference.'

'Time has no meaning when it comes to instinct. You're passionate about the work you do. That all-encompassing passion had to stem from somewhere.'

'We all have pasts that shape us, Your Highness,' she

responded stiltedly, not wanting to recall the volatile quagmire she and her siblings had lived in before her parents' final showdown had ended everything.

'I agree. Tell me that shaping didn't involve anything physical and I'll drop the subject.'

Her eyes widened as she stared at him and noted the naked intensity in his eyes.

Mouth dry, she shook her head. 'No, I wasn't physically abused.'

He exhaled and gave a grim nod.

They flew in silence for a few more minutes, during which time Allegra dragged her mind from the painful past to the present. Below her, more evidence of Dar-Aman's devastated infrastructure sprawled in derelict abandonment. But among it, several new buildings were springing up, evidence of the rebirth Rahim had mentioned.

It didn't stop her from mourning the majestic loss, though.

He glanced at her as she sighed.

'You mentioned your grandfather, but not your parents. Are they involved in the charity too?' Rahim's voice piped through her headphones.

Her heart lurched at the mention of her parents. 'I thought you were going to drop the subject?' she demanded.

Rahim's mouth twisted in a curiously empathetic ghost of a smile. 'Easy, *habibi*. I will let it be if you wish me to.'

The unexpected statement of understanding loosened something inside her. Coupled with all the roiling emotions churning through her, she wasn't surprised when she found herself confessing, 'My parents died when I was six.'

He gave another nod but didn't spout the inane sympathies most people did on the rare occasion she talked about her parents.

'I guess that's one unfortunate thing we have in common.'

Allegra frowned. 'I thought… Didn't your father pass away only six months ago?'

Rahim's jaw tightened, his impassive eyes focused on the horizon ahead. 'He did, but in many ways he was dead long before he drew his last breath.'

She wanted to ask what he meant. Then deny that they had anything in common. But Allegra was reeling from the overwhelming realisation of just how much she'd bared herself to Rahim Al-Hadi in so short a time. And none of those revelations had got her closer to completing the task her grandfather had set her.

She was grappling with a way to tackle the subject when they soared over a steep hill.

'What's that?' She indicated the construction site beneath her.

'The new racing track to be completed by the end of the year. We host our first top-tier race here next spring.'

Allegra struggled to keep her emotions in check. 'Did I read somewhere that you were a racer?' she bit out.

'Only on amateur circuits. The situation of my birth precludes me from placing myself in such a dangerous profession,' he replied with a shrug of acceptance and regret.

'But you own supercars, don't you?'

He nodded, then glanced at her with a slight frown. 'Several. What's your point? And don't tell me there isn't one, because I hear an ocean of judgement in your voice. Are you going to accuse me of not caring about my people again?'

'Do you?' She searched his face, wondering why his answer meant so much to her.

'Of course,' he replied, his voice deep and unwavering. 'I don't believe in throwing money at a problem until I know the root cause of it.'

'From where I'm standing the root cause of your country's problems is very easy to see. You may be doing something *now*, but it begs the question why no one outside of your precious palace has cared enough *until* now. If they had, your kingdom wouldn't be in this state.'

A grunt of disbelief echoed through her headphone, followed a deathly silence where she only heard the echo of her own voice. A quick glance behind her showed degrees of horror on the faces of the bodyguards before they quickly averted their gazes.

God, what had she done?

Clenching her fists in her lap, she tried to scramble for something to mitigate the bomb she'd just thrown in her own way.

Chagrined, she took several deep breaths. Rahim Al-Hadi got under her skin with an ease that was frightening. And yet she knew she'd stepped over the line. Way over the line. 'Your Highness…'

'You've said enough for now, Miss Di Sione. While I do not wish to bore you with the protocols of my country, I need to warn you that further insults aimed at me will result in your arrest, or worse. So perhaps you need to curb any more observations until we're alone?'

Before she could attempt to bumble her way through yet another explanation to excuse her runaway tongue, he banked the chopper, this time heading west and away from the dazzling waters of the Arabian Sea.

The terrain below swiftly changed from lush greenery to shrub land before merging seamlessly into the undulations of the Dar-Aman desert. Silence fell within the aircraft as the rotors whipped through the hot air.

When one of the bodyguards leaned forward and

pointed, Rahim nodded and started to descend towards the convoy of sturdy SUVs lined up on a flat clearing.

The moment they landed a group in traditional Berber garb, led by an old man who was clearly the elder, strode forward. His wizened face creased in a smile as he hugged Rahim, then kissed him on both cheeks, before touching his hand to his heart several times.

Slowly stepping down from the chopper, Allegra observed the welcoming gestures—which she knew from her cultural interactions were reserved for revered guests and family. After several minutes, Rahim looked over to where she stood. In an instant the cordial expression melted from his face.

Without speaking, he nodded to one of his men, who came forward and indicated that she get into one of the many SUVs.

The realisation that she wouldn't be travelling with Rahim brought sharp, disconcerting disappointment that threw her for a stunned second. She plastered a smile on her face when she noticed curious eyes turned on her. Silently, she took her seat. The smile was quickly wiped from her face when the convoy raced away from the choppers, taking a terrain that convinced her she'd broken more than one bone in her body by the time the rough, turbulent half-hour ride came to a halt on the fringe of a group of canvas-brown Bedouin tents. From either side of the settlement craggy mountains rose, and Allegra understood the need for ditching the choppers to make the final leg of the journey by land.

The scene was spectacular, if more than a little rough on her bones. Gingerly she got out of the car. And found Rahim standing in front of her.

'Are you all right?' he asked.

His large frame vibrated with an icy anger that told Allegra her outburst in the chopper remained very much an issue between them. It surprised her that he was going out of his way to enquire about her comfort considering he was very displeased with her.

'I'm fine. Listen, about what I said…'

He gave a firm shake of his head. 'We will discuss this later.'

Rahim bit out instructions in Arabic and all but two women and the elder remained. At his further instructions the women rushed forward and bowed. 'Laila and Sharifa will take you to get cleaned up and serve you some refreshments. We will return to the palace once my meeting is over.'

He started to walk away.

'Your Highness…'

He whirled abruptly towards her. 'You seem intent on drawing quite severe conclusions about me. Am I really so irredeemable?'

The direct question and the fact that he seemed genuinely puzzled by her observations took her aback. Since she had no answer that would be diplomatic enough, she countered it with one of her own. 'Why are you so keen for me to take an interest in you?'

He tensed slightly, but then shrugged. 'How else will you set aside your prejudged bias and see the light?'

'I'm not reacting to anything that's not right in front of me.' Knowing her response was directed more at him than at his kingdom sent a wave of shame through her.

His dark brows clamped beneath the shade of his *keffiyeh*. For several heartbeats he just stared at her. 'Perhaps this wasn't a good idea after all,' he mused darkly. He nodded to the ladies hovering nearby. 'I will be done in two hours and we'll return to the palace.'

He was gone before she could reply.

When the women stepped forward and indicated that

she follow them, Allegra sighed inwardly and summoned another smile.

An hour later, after an attempt to ride a disgruntled camel, and a short trail up several sand dunes to a point between two distant mountains to witness the most spectacular sunset, she washed her hands and feet, and sat cross-legged on a plump, richly embroidered cushion in a cool, stunningly decorated tent.

The half a dozen women who crowded around her spoke varying degrees of English, and Allegra was shocked to find that most of them had been pursuing academic careers at one point in their lives. Careers that had come to an abrupt halt around the same time about fifteen years ago.

Her tentative queries as to why drew dismissive shrugs, then furtive glances and lapses into heated Dar-Amanian when Allegra probed further.

Realising she'd broached a touchy issue, she attempted to change the subject only to clamp her mouth shut when her nape prickled with the keen awareness that she was under scrutiny.

The finger she'd been absently licking froze on her lower lip as her head snapped up and her gaze collided with Rahim's.

He glanced from her face to her fingers, then to the empty dishes spread out before her, the icy look in his eyes emphasised by his cocked brow.

'Dare I venture that the past two hours haven't been pure torture for you?'

Allegra reddened. 'Not entirely,' she replied.

'It's time to return to the palace. That is, of course, if you can bear to tear yourself away.'

He stood watching in brooding silence as she washed her hands and stood. Again his expression was a mixture of anger and puzzlement.

The moment she reached him, he turned and strode out, his stature and billowing robe cutting an imperious figure through the crowd gathered to wave their sheikh off.

As she quickened her steps after him, Allegra found herself admitting she didn't like silent and brooding Rahim Al-Hadi.

Not one little bit.

CHAPTER FIVE

BY THE TIME the helicopter landed back on the rolling green lawns of Dar-Aman Palace, Allegra was near-ready to jump out of the charged atmosphere. Rahim had barely made conversation, only answering direct questions she posed. His answers weren't monosyllabic, but from the terse responses, they may as well have been.

'Why were you meeting with the elders?' She asked the question that had been hovering on her lips since they took off from Nur-Aman.

For a second, she thought he wouldn't answer her. But Rahim glanced down at her as they neared the hallway that led to her suite. She breathed a sigh of relief when his steps slowed to match hers. She dismissed the part of her that mocked her for delaying the return to the crassly named *women's wing*. Or that she was searching for further redeeming qualities of the man who'd run his kingdom to the ground while keeping himself draped in priceless arts and fast cars.

'Did you notice the abandoned pipelines that were laid close to the tribe encampment?' he asked.

'Yes,' she answered.

'That mountain was where my first ancestor discovered the malachite that Dar-Aman is renowned for. In the valley below Nur-Aman is where we struck our first crude deposit. Those pipes were laid almost twenty years ago. It was a bold and brilliant plan that should've brought jobs and sustainable revenue growth to the Nur-Aman people.'

The deep pride in his voice enthralled her, while making her wonder why he'd remained blind to the needs of his people until recently.

'But?'

'But they haven't been touched for over fifteen years.'

'I could tell. Why not?'

Rahim's expression showed mingled displeasure and bitterness. Wondering where the latter emotion had come from, she waited for him to answer.

'Contracts were renegotiated and the oil drilling concerns sold off to faceless foreign corporations.'

'Aren't there laws to prevent that from happening?'

He shrugged. 'They were bent far enough but not broken.'

She pursed her lips. 'I'm surprised you would freely admit something like that.'

'I have nothing to hide, Allegra. Especially not about something as important as this.'

'What are you going to do about it?'

'There's only one course of action. I intend to get back, and keep, what is mine.'

Staring into his eyes, Allegra grew hot all over, absurdly affected by words that pertained to oil rights and furthering his riches.

But it was there all the same, fuelling a whole heap of confusion.

They reached the doors of her suite, and Rahim threw them open. Nura was nowhere to be seen and Allegra's heart began a discordant hammer as she walked into the living room, followed closely by Rahim, and his overwhelmingly masculine presence.

'Well, thank you for bringing me along. It was certainly an eye-opening experience,' she said when she'd ran out of

places to direct her attention and finally looked in his face
to find him watching her with an intensity that dragged
more heat through her stomach.

It took monumental willpower to tear her gaze from the
sensual curve of his mouth.

He prowled to where she stood and caught an errant curl
that had escaped her ponytail. Thoughtfully, with unhurried movements, he rubbed the strands between his fingers before tucking it behind her ear.

The electrifying touch, though it whispered over her
skin for a few seconds, sent wild and fiery currents racing through her. Allegra's stomach clenched in reaction
to the arrows of fiery arousal lancing her. She forced herself to swallow when her mouth filled with a longing she
couldn't describe. When his hand fell to his side, it was
all she could do not to catch and pull it back up to repeat
the caress.

'I'm glad your eyes have been opened.'

'Are…are you?' she asked vaguely, still yearning for his
touch with a hunger that scared and surprised her.

As if he'd read her thoughts, his hand slowly lifted. This
time he caressed her cheek, then her jaw, his touch almost
reverent as it traced her skin. When he reached the corner
of her mouth, Allegra held her breath, almost too afraid
to move in case he removed it. 'Of course. It would please
me even more if you applied your observations fruitfully.
Can I count on you to do that, Allegra?'

Knowing she should be giving this conversation better
attention, she tried to focus, but his thumb, now tracing
her lower lip, threatened to send her reasoning into free
fall. 'I'm not sure…what…'

He placed a stalling finger on her lips. 'I have a proposition to make to you, Allegra. One I sincerely hope you'll
be receptive to.' His eyes burned as he looked down at her.

She'd seen that look once, in a movie when the male

lead actor had made an indecent proposal to the actress. At the time, she'd silently scoffed at the improbability of it all. Now, with her breath lodged in her throat, Allegra waited, an almost forbidden excitement racing through her blood. When he said nothing after a few minutes, she cleared her throat. 'What…what sort of proposition?' she asked huskily, every sensitive nerve ending on her mouth reacting to the brush of his finger.

His beautiful eyes darkened, the hunger that clawed through her emblazoned boldly in his gaze. 'One that I hope will align our goals now that you've spent some time in Dar-Aman.' Once again his finger trailed over her skin. This time it wove a path down her jaw to her shoulder, then drifted down her arm to capture her hand. Catching her fingers with his, he brought her hand to his lips to kiss her knuckles. A smile tilted the corner of his mouth when she gasped. 'We will talk further this evening. The banquet starts at eight. I will collect you shortly before then.'

He turned and walked out, leaving her in a state of sensual confusion and hyped excitement. And despite telling herself she was a fool to fall into such an obvious trap, Allegra couldn't summon a practical enough argument to calm her racing pulse as she walked into her bedroom in a daze to undress.

Rahim strode away from Allegra's suite with a burning in his bloodstream and the knowledge that the game had altered significantly. Not enough to sway him from what he needed to do for his people. More like the dimensions of his intentions had grown, while the prototype remained the same.

It wasn't a dynamic he altogether welcomed, because he'd never been one to mix business with pleasure. Or let his personal urges get in the way of his ultimate goals. Sex with Allegra, no matter how detached he would choose to view it, would be personal enough to jeopardise what she and her foundation could do for Dar-Aman.

Because to put it simply, he wanted to bed Allegra Di Sione. He'd known it from the moment he looked into her enthralling eyes this morning. Even through her wild and unfounded tirades, he'd found himself pulled closer to the powerful attraction that tugged fiercely between them.

For a while this afternoon, though, he'd been sure he'd made a mistake in thinking she could be the answer to his problems. He'd been set to send her packing the moment they returned, but then she'd started asking him questions on the chopper. Even then he'd been sceptical. Her interest in what he was doing at Nur-Aman had been the convincer he needed to slam the brakes on putting her on the first plane out of Dar-Aman. Perhaps his trip hadn't been fruitless after all. She'd taken an interest, and that was something he could work with.

Rahim knew without conceit that, with further work, he could knock a few holes in her preconceived notions about him, and he planned to use that leverage to his every advantage.

As for the crackling attraction between them... He let out a frustrated groan at the tightening in his groin.

Despite the intelligence that shone from her eyes and the monumental public success of her foundation, Allegra Di Sione had all the hallmarks of a high-maintenance woman in private. Beneath her practical and stoic demeanour, he'd glimpsed a passionate temper, one that could flare out of control if not handled correctly.

Rahim didn't intend to be the one to handle her in that capacity. He'd had enough experience of high-maintenance women to last him a lifetime. His footsteps slowed as he neared his private rooms. All around him were signs of his mother—in the wide alcove overlooking her favourite garden where she'd kept exotic birds for her amusement, to the sitting rooms decorated with priceless rugs, tapestries and cabinets full of delicate trinkets. Everywhere he looked memories flooded him of her huge, all-encompassing smile when her father presented her with a jewelled ornament after a business trip, or her diva tantrum when a whimsical wish wasn't fulfilled immediately.

It was a failing to nitpick his mother, but while Rahim had known he was loved with absolute devotion as a child, he'd experienced a period of abject fear of what his life would be like were that the love be taken away when he'd had a taster of it on his eleventh birthday.

His first vow not to allow love or any emotions resembling it into his life had been uttered that night. It had grown to spurn any overtures remotely resembling it as he grew older. Sex he could deal with. Hell, he'd made it a life choice to indulge in affairs of the flesh even while he conceded that his earliest forays into his shocking lifestyle had been mostly to get his father's attention.

A sad and bitter truth he still had a hard time swallowing.

Another truth he didn't want to admit was that if Allegra was to be his saviour, then sex had to be taken off the table.

The pressure in his groin protested at that edict. Ignoring it, Rahim walked through the carved double doors that led to his bedchamber, and out onto his private terrace. He glanced to the left to where the women's wing was located. His fingers tingled in wild recollection of Allegra's silky skin and luscious mouth beneath his touch. The need to taste her had been urgent in the extreme. But it was a weakness he had to master.

Perhaps in the future, once his kingdom was on firmer ground and his leadership wasn't in doubt, he could pick things up with her...

He shook his head and fisted the tingle from his fingers.

Turning abruptly, he strolled to the west wing, the parts that overlooked the grand ballroom, where preparations were being made for the banquet tonight. Exhaling, he accepted that there was really no choice, not when it came to his people.

Their welfare came first and foremost. Selfish needs of the flesh, no matter how bone-crushingly desperate, would have to take second place.

Rahim scrambled to find that keen sense of duty when Allegra opened the door to his knock ninety minutes later.

Fire swept through his veins as he fought to control his breathing. Dressed in a fitted floor-length gown of the deepest azure that almost exactly matched her eyes, and heels that brought her height to his chin, she was a vision of regal beauty that stole his breath away.

'Good evening,' she murmured.

He returned the greeting; then, because he couldn't seem to help himself, he uttered the words burning on his tongue. 'You look exquisitely beautiful.'

Colour flared beneath her skin in a delicate blush, and she smiled. Rahim's fingers tingled again with the need to touch, to caress.

'Thank you. You don't look so bad yourself.'

Her hair was styled in layered waves caught on one side by a diamond pin, flowing over her shoulder on the other. The curls he'd spotted in her ponytail earlier were more pronounced now and he had to fight every instinct not to plunge his hand into the rich tresses and test their silky luxury for himself. Preferably a prelude to pulling her close to plunder the peach-coloured gloss that sheened her luscious mouth.

Cursing the gods for the ill-timed bout of lust he couldn't suppress, he forced a smile, thankful his robe concealed the evidence of his arousal.

'As we're a little early, we'll take the more picturesque route to the ballroom.'

He tensed in expectation of her protest. When she readily nodded, Rahim breathed easier. 'I'd like that. I've been reading a bit more about the fascinating history of the palace, especially the interior decorations. I'd really love to see more of it, if you don't mind?'

Rahim told himself he should be pleased she was taking a keener interest, and yet the somewhat superficial request made him grimace inwardly, reminding him of past female conquests who'd attempted to impress him with their knowledge of all things Dar-Aman, unknowingly triggering their swift exit from his life. Besides that, Allegra's furtive glance sparked something within him that he couldn't put his finger on.

Brushing the feeling away, he reminded himself of the bigger picture. 'Of course. We'll start in the bazaar room. I'm told it's the most photographed room in this part of the world.'

Relief tinged her voice, prompting the spark to escalate, but her words seemed harmless enough. 'Thank you. I had hoped you wouldn't hold my earlier lack of grace against me.' Her smile was wide and alluring and Rahim cautioned himself not to be drawn into it.

'I would be a fool not to forgive, especially if I hope for you to leave with a better impression of me than you arrived with.'

She glanced at him, her lower lip caught between her teeth. Rahim fought to suppress a groan.

'The night's still young. Let's not be too hasty,' she replied wryly.

Rahim sighed with a touch of melodrama. 'Here I was hoping to enthrall everyone with my utterly adorable personality by the time the appetisers were served.'

Her laugh lit up a dark and cold place within him, and it was all he could do not to stop and drink in the sound.

'Next you'll be calling yourself cute and cuddly.'

One arrogant brow quirked, he shook his head. 'You're right, let's not be too hasty.'

It seemed the most natural thing in the world then to offer her his arm. Her hesitation was brief but she slid her slender arm through his and fell into step beside him.

The delicate scent of her perfume engulfed them as he walked her out of the east wing. They were approaching the bazaar room when she stopped. 'That's incredible.'

Following the direction of her gaze, he smiled at her reaction to the centrepiece in the atrium, which sat directly underneath the central golden dome.

The solid white marble statue of the horse was surrounded by twelve cherubs wielding large flutes that spewed water into the fountain. The Arabian stallion was displayed in all his magnificent male glory, its wild and thick mane flowing in powerful abandon as it reared out of the water on its hind legs.

When she started to drift towards the fountain, Rahim lifted a hand and dismissed his trailing bodyguards. Their footsteps faded away until the only sound in the space was the splashing of the water.

'That was my mother's favourite horse,' Rahim found himself confessing. 'When he died in a racing accident, my father had this memorial built for her.'

She walked around the statue, examining it with wide-eyed fascination. When she reached the front of it, her fingers caressed the words carved in stone. 'What does this mean?'

'It translates loosely as *Cherished One*.'

A small smile lifted her mouth, one tinged with sadness a part of him recognised and commiserated with.

'Every inch of this place is unbelievably breathtaking, almost like a fairy tale.'

Rahim tried to hide his bitterness as he answered. 'That was the purpose behind the design. My mother wanted a fairy-tale palace. My father made sure she got exactly what she wanted.'

'It is truly beautiful. A magical place.' Her words were genuine, and Rahim saw her soft smile as she traced her fingers over the words once more. 'Your father must have loved her very much if he moved heaven and earth to give her what she wanted?'

The seething sadness and underlying anger he felt when he thought about his father rose higher. 'I guess you could say that.'

Allegra paused in her examination of the statue and glanced at him. 'Oh? You didn't see it that way?'

He shrugged. 'Some would see it as love, I guess. Others might see it as an obsession that was detrimental in the long run.'

'And you're one of those who believe in the latter?'

Words he didn't want to say locked in his throat. But the moment seemed to take over, the urge to share, to unburden surging from nowhere and catapulting the words from him.

'Come with me.'

Her eyes widened. 'Where?'

Rahim shook his head. 'It'll only take a moment.' He caught her hand, his gut tensing at the sizzling contact.

His footsteps slowed as he reached the double doors that led to the north wing. Throwing it open, he flicked on the light and watched it bathe the plum and gold decor. Like elsewhere in the palace, the sweeping marble staircase was the centrepiece, designed for a princess to descend in grace and elegance.

'Wow, I really can't get over this place.'

Rahim, beginning to doubt his sanity in exposing himself to such disturbing memories, only nodded.

Perhaps alerted to his altered mood, Allegra completed the full admiring circle and faced him. 'Why did you bring me here, Rahim?'

He let himself glance at the stairs. 'You know why this wing is closed?'

'No, there was no mention of it in the book…'

'Of course not. That book is made for believers in fairy tales.' She frowned at his thick cynicism, but didn't interrupt. Only watched him as Rahim was assailed with the sudden need to pace.

'My mother was rushing down those stairs to show my father a new ornament she'd bought when she tripped and fell. She suffered a concussion and a broken ankle and fell into a brief coma.'

He barely heard Allegra's murmur of horror, caught up in the memory of those harrowing days and the real fear struck into his heart when he'd seen just how love could weaken a strong and noble man, a man he'd hitherto thought invincible.

'Overnight, my father became a useless mess, neglecting everything and everyone, including his own confused and frightened son, as he'd mounted a vigil at my mother's bedside.'

'How long was she ill for?'

'She was in hospital for six days. During that time I was allowed to visit her only once for five minutes. My father was terrified she could get an infection, despite the doctor's assurances otherwise. He shut the whole world out, completely. The times when he was forced to partake in affairs of state, he would go through the motions with almost zombie-like animation. I heard some of his aides whispering about his mental state more than a few times in that week.'

'But your mother got better?'

He whirled away from her, from the stairs that symbolised so many things he wanted to forget.

'She came home. And aside from my father closing the north wing so he didn't have to see where she fell, yes, things got better. But things were never the same.'

'Because you witnessed the depth of your parents' love?' Allegra ventured, a gentle but haunting understanding on her face as she stared at him.

'No. I saw the *destructiveness* of my father's *obsession*.'

Rahim's eyes had been wrenched wide open to the debilitating effects of love. The emotion he'd basked in and taken for granted had suddenly been what he'd feared would be his own and his beloved homeland's eventual downfall.

'But even then I hoped I was wrong. That what I'd witnessed from my father that week had been a temporary aberration.' Because surely his father's love was supposed to envelope his son and every single one of his subjects, not just his beloved wife? And that love should empower him to be a better ruler and father, not a hollowed-out wraith the moment it was threatened?

'What happened?' she asked from behind him.

'My mother died four years later and my father proved to me just how much worse things could get.'

One hand slid over his bicep, pressing, surprising him with its strength. Surprising him with how much he wanted it to remain there. 'You must have both been devastated.'

'My father's life ended that day.' Khalil Al-Hadi had stopped living the moment his wife and unborn second child had died. 'And as soon as I was able, I moved to Washington, DC.' It was the place he'd forced himself to call home. The place he'd used the next fifteen years to forget his father and his homeland.

At first, Rahim hadn't wanted to believe what was playing out before his very eyes. But with each day, he'd seen his reality alter alarmingly and his life slip into a frightening hell that triggered unfortunate reactions in him. By the time he'd realised his attempts were futile, that his father could see no further than his absolute grief, Rahim's hedonistic lifestyle had become an addiction he hadn't wanted to shake. He'd seen no reason to put the brakes on the heady freedom that came with little or no responsibility with matters concerning Dar-Aman. After all, if his father couldn't be bothered to take an interest in what Rahim did, Rahim would reciprocate by cutting himself off totally from his homeland.

He rubbed absently at the pain lodged beneath his collarbone, his soul mourning just how effective his self-imposed exile had been. So much so he hadn't known how bad things got…how badly his people had been neglected.

'There's more to it than that though, isn't there?'

His mouth twisted in a caricature of a smile as he turned to face her. He stared into her clear blue eyes, wondering what it would feel like to drown in them. Collecting himself, he stalled for time. 'There always is, *habibi*, as I believe there is for you too. But this is where I cop out and say I don't wish to speak ill of the dead.'

'Or this is where you show a chink in your armour that says you're human.'

'Why would I want to display such a flaw?'

'Aren't heroes with flaws the ones who always win the girl in the end? Or am I misquoting popular fiction?'

'We're not fictional characters, Allegra,' he stated matter-of-factly. 'Blind obsession can be harmful to the giver and the receiver. I prefer to live in reality, no matter how unpalatable it can be at times.'

His observation blew away the last of the lingering wistfulness in her eyes. He watched, fascinated, as her practical façade slid into place. 'You're right, we're not living in a fairy tale. Shall we continue with the tour?'

Like a true diplomat, she made the right noises, and admired the rich frescoes and endless rows of jaw-dropping chandeliers once they reached the bazaar room, but after examining a few ornaments set on the long sideboards lining the walls, she was ready to move on. The library that had been his grandfather's pride and joy also received praise, but it wasn't until they reached the throne room, where all the coronations in Dar-Aman had taken place, that her eyes lit up with true interest.

'All the crowns from the very first ruler of Dar-Aman are kept in this room.'

'If I remember correctly, it's also the room that holds your mother's most extensive collection of antique treasure boxes, correct?'

He smiled. 'Correct, although there's another smaller, private collection,' he replied.

Before he could give a further history, she let go of his arm and moved to the first cabinet. Rahim watched her carefully examine each ornament, enquire as to its pedigree before moving to the next.

He offered further snippets of information, but she seemed oblivious to him, her engrossment in the cabinets complete.

When a discreet cough alerted him to Harun's presence, he turned. Nodding at his advisor's silent signal, Rahim turned to her. 'Your presence as guest of honour is required.'

She hid her disappointment well, but he saw it. 'Can we return later?'

'If you wish,' he murmured, his instinct sending a veiled warning he couldn't quite decipher yet. She didn't take his arm again, and she seemed almost reluctant to leave the throne room.

When they reached the Mariam Ballroom, named after his grandmother, he made it a point to introduce her to as many dignitaries as possible. Allegra conversed intelligently, but through it all Rahim could sense her distraction, like she was wearing a mask that she was growing weary of donning.

Puzzled, he tried harder to engage her, to steer her round to what he wanted to discuss with her. It was only when he mentioned the women of Nur-Aman that she focused fully on him.

'Are you going to put a new system in place for their education?' she demanded after taking a bite of her sweetened fig dessert.

'It's in my plans to make that happen within the year. I'm also in talks with other communities in and out of Shar-el-Aman too.'

'I'm glad to hear that,' she said.

Rahim nodded, thankful she'd finally got on track. 'Not just the women, but for the children especially. But before I do that I need to attend to my personal…image overhaul.'

She frowned. 'What has your personal image got to do with anything?'

Rahim paused, knowing he'd reached the delicate part of his negotiations. 'A lot, as you probably know.'

Her spoon clattered to her plate. 'Only if you intend to put your self-interest above that of your people,' she replied sharply enough to turn a few heads.

Rahim smiled at their audience through gritted teeth, then rose from the table. The sign that the banquet was officially over sent his guests rising to their feet. Unfortunately, it also meant a slight prolonging of his hosting duties as he put an end to the celebration.

By the time he finished making sufficient rounds to satisfy protocol, Allegra stood stiffly to one side, a plastic smile stretched across her face. When he reached her, he bent low and whispered tersely in her ear.

'Let's go and have that talk now.'

At her stiff nod, he steered her out of the ballroom, aware that they were the cynosure of numerous eyes, but frankly uncaring too much of what they thought. He'd been right in thinking she was high maintenance. Already he'd grown tired of walking on eggshells around her, and the certainty that he needed her to help restore his image was fast being chipped away by the frustration eating at him.

His office was the nearest private room. He dismissed the aide who was stationed in the outer office and ushered Allegra into his large office.

Shutting the door behind him, he led her to a leather sofa grouped before a window overlooking his private courtyard. Once she was seated, he paced before her, suddenly at a loss at how to handle this without it blowing up in his face.

He was so lost in composing the right words in his head that he didn't realise minutes had gone by.

'Rahim?'

His name on her lips stopped him in his tracks. Inhaling deeply, he said, 'It is clear that your reasons for coming to Dar-Aman don't seem to collide with mine, but there's no reason why we can't make this work.'

A frown gathered between her brows. 'I... What? I don't understand...'

Rushing forward, he sat down next to her, then immediately acknowledged what a mistake that was. This close, he could see the rise and fall of her chest beneath the band of her bodice and the shadow of her cleavage was a sight he couldn't drag his gaze from.

He forced his eyes up, and continued. 'I know it's not what you normally do, but I'm willing to foot the bill for that aspect of your work.'

Her frown intensified. 'Sorry, I really have no clue what you're getting at.'

Rahim gritted his teeth. 'I'm not sure whether you're deliberately being obtuse or...' He stopped and took a breath. 'You're here on behalf of the Di Sione Foundation. I'm aware of the broad parameters of the foundation's requirements. All it would take is a little streamlining to include PR work. If it's payment you're worried about, I'll see to it that you're fully remunerated for all your efforts.'

Her mouth dropped opened in a bewildered O, then firmed again as she fought to find the words. To refuse him most likely. A wave of futile anger spread through Rahim but he pushed it down. His personal feelings didn't matter here. All that mattered was that she agreed to help him to help his people.

Before he could plead his case further she blurted, 'I came to Dar-Aman because you have a box in your possession. A Fabergé box. I wish to purchase it from you. That's my only reason for being here. If you would be so kind as to name your price, I'll arrange for payment before I leave tomorrow.'

CHAPTER SIX

ALLEGRA WATCHED SEVERAL emotions criss-cross Rahim's face. Then his brow thundered together in an incandescent frown. 'A...*box*? You made this trip for the sake of a box?' Puzzled disbelief hollowed his voice.

'Yes. But it's not just any box, I assure you. It has special meaning to someone very close to me.'

He reeled back in his seat, shock still lingering on his face, before he surged to his feet. 'Let me get this straight. Your visit here has *nothing* to do with the Di Sione Foundation or the Dar-Aman people?' he blazed at her, his eyes so dark they were almost bronze.

She swallowed, knowing she skated on very dangerous ground and needed to tread carefully. 'My foundation may have an interest in Dar-Aman in the future. I'm willing to look at a proposal from you, but for now my immediate need is the box...'

'*May*...in the *distant future*?' His voice was cold to the point of freezing. 'So you came here and took pleasure in condemning my kingdom just for the sake of your own amusement?'

'No, that's not why I came here, but I can't just switch off who I am because I'm not officially on duty. The foundation is not just my job. It's my life.'

'Then prove it.'

She bristled. 'I don't need to prove anything to you...' Her words trailed off when he emphatically shook his head.

'You had no intention of setting up your work here to help with restoring Dar-Aman's profile, did you?'

'You speak of restoring profiles and PR campaigns. That's not what the Di Sione Foundation does. For what you want you'd be better off hiring a PR company. Perhaps my sister Bianca's company can be more useful to you?'

A flash of colour scoured his cheekbones and his jaw gritted tightly before he answered. 'I'm aware of what your foundation does. I'm also aware that what I'm suggesting isn't an alien concept to you. You've done it before in the past.'

He gave two examples and Allegra had to concede he'd done his homework, albeit in a slightly convoluted way. 'You're right, but that was for an outfit geared towards rehabilitating a disaster-struck zone, not for a playboy billionaire who suddenly wants to play at being ruler to a kingdom on the brink of regaining its rightful place as a superpower after a shaky period.'

Rahim went rigid. Anger vibrated from his body, and Allegra closed her eyes for a second in regret, knowing she'd just blown any chance of securing her grandfather's precious box out of the water.

'I assure you, I've never *played* at being anything in my life. And the state of Dar-Aman's infrastructure is the way I inherited it when I ascended to the throne six months ago…'

'And you've turned things round since you took the throne but you were the crown prince from the day you were born!'

The smile that touched Rahim's lips was as icy as his regard. 'I thought you did your homework, Miss Di Sione? Obviously not since you're not aware of such a common piece of information. Until six months ago I hadn't set foot in Dar-Aman for fifteen years.'

Shock drenched her at the news, even as she flinched at

the formal clip of her name. 'So…you're saying your father was responsible for the state of affairs in your kingdom, not you? You didn't think as crown prince that you owed your people your care and attention your presence in Dar-Aman would've given them, especially knowing the state your father was in?'

His head snapped back as if she'd struck him, then he glared icily down his aristocratic nose at her. 'Be very careful about the insults you fling around. I have never absolved myself of my contribution to the neglect my people have suffered. I chose to absent myself, so all I can do is try to pick up the pieces.'

Allegra heard the thread of hollow bleakness in his tone, and her heart lurched as she was reminded of her own impending loss. The thought of her grandfather spurred her to her feet.

'But I'm still ruler in this kingdom, and as my guest, you owe me your respect.'

Shame washed over her. 'I'm sorry.'

His eyes narrowed. 'For what exactly are you sorry?'

'For your people's suffering, of course. But, Rahim…'

He stiffened. 'Since we're no longer cordial, you will address me as Your Highness.'

She sucked in a sustaining breath. 'I… Your Highness, I would still like to discuss the box, if…'

Rahim volleyed an imprecation in Arabic. 'Unbelievable! You think you can soften me up with a false show of sympathy right before you demand what you truly came here for?'

She gasped. 'That wasn't false!'

His hand slashed through the air with deadly impatience. 'Why should I believe you when it's clear you came here under false pretences?'

'What?'

'You told me on the phone that you were coming to Dar-

Aman in your capacity as the head of the Di Sione…' He stopped suddenly, and laughed. The sound was like fingernails on a chalkboard. 'Very clever to trick me with your words. Tell me, do you always get away with this kind of subtle subterfuge?'

Allegra's face flamed, knowing very well it was what she'd done. 'Please…this is important.'

'As are my people to me, Miss Di Sione. And by wasting time with you, I've set myself back even further from making real progress.'

She jumped to her feet, desperation clawing higher and harder by the second. 'Rahim,' she started, but paused when she saw his set jaw. 'Your Highness, I'll offer you whatever you want for the box.'

He regarded her for a full, disbelieving minute. Then he strolled forward until he was a single foot from her. This close, she could feel the turbulent emotions vibrating from his hard body. It took a huge amount of strength not to step back from him.

'You travelled thousands of miles for the sake of a trinket.' The mild sneer was mingled with something else. Something that sounded curiously like bitterness. 'It really means that much to you?'

She didn't waste time wondering why he would be bitter about her intentions. 'Yes.'

'And you expect me to drop everything to help you on this whimsical quest?'

'Well, I…'

'It seems we're both to be losers in this little tale. You never had any intention of offering me the services of your foundation, and I have better things to do than to chase after little trinkets. Even you will agree that my time is better suited elsewhere?' He flicked a glance at his wrist and continued without waiting for an answer. 'It's late, and seeing as I've wasted precious time with you that I could ill afford, I must get back to work. I will have an aide escort you to your chambers. A driver will take you to the airport in the morning. You and I will not meet again.'

He started to walk away. Panic held Allegra rigid before she wrenched herself out of it. 'You'll deny an old man his dying wish?'

He froze with his hand on the doorknob, then turned with a grace that was fascinating to behold. 'Excuse me?'

'The box…it's for my grandfather. It belonged to him a long time ago. Please, he's dying, you see…'

If she'd expected sympathy or any softening, she got the opposite. Rahim's face hardened until it was a stony, hauntingly beautiful statue. But his eyes were alive with pure, incandescent condemnation.

'If there's one thing I detest more than subterfuge, it's emotional manipulation. Trust me when I say, you've just destroyed any chance of getting what you wanted. Even if I felt inclined to go hunting for an ornament in a palace full of thousands of them—which I don't—you've assured yourself an even firmer refusal. Goodnight.'

He left, leaving behind a seething silence disturbed only by her rough, stunned breathing.

She'd failed.

The gnawing realisation made her double over, her heart hammering loud in her ears as she fought not to hyperventilate. Visions of how the conversation would go with her grandfather reeled across her mind as she stumbled back to the chair and dropped her head into her hands.

As close as she was to her grandfather, she knew he'd found her lacking in most things except the running of her foundation. The thought of returning empty-handed, telling him that she'd screwed up what could be his last request of her, and severely angered the ruler of a powerful kingdom to boot, wrenched a despairing sob from her.

Allegra had no idea how long she sat there staring into

the lamplit distance. She didn't know the story behind the box Giovanni wanted back so desperately, but the look in his eyes when he'd pleaded with her to find it was stamped vividly in her memory. Her eyes prickled, but she dashed the tears away.

She'd failed this time, but she refused to believe all was lost. Perhaps what she needed was to give Rahim time for his anger towards her to cool. Or she could make him a better offer.

Determinedly, she stood, but a few steps later she faltered. What had she to give except a tainted proffer of help after she'd condemned him so thoroughly? Anything she suggested now would be soured and firmly refused.

Biting her lip, she paced the floor in front of the sofa, discarding each idea she came up with as weak and useless. Rahim would see through every ploy to secure the box now he believed she'd come to Dar-Aman under false pretences. About to leave the office, she stopped to pick up the wrap she'd dropped on the sofa, and saw the glossy coffee table book. She picked up the publication, the title—*The Treasures of Dar-Aman*—jumping at her. The name of the world-renowned photographer/author leapt out at her and she knew that he wouldn't have left a stone unturned in documenting everything that was worth documenting.

Hands shaking, Allegra dropped back on the sofa and turned the first page. Quickly scanning the table of contents, her breath snagged in her lungs when she saw the subtitle—*For the Love of Fabergé.*

Flipping over to the relevant page, she speed-read the introduction. Rahim's mother had possessed a weakness for trinket boxes, especially priceless ones with rich histories. Objets d'art from the House of Fabergé had been her particular favourite and she'd been an avid collector from a very young age. Once she'd married, her husband had made it his personal mission to gift her with as many boxes as possible.

Allegra scanned the pictures. On the third page, she stopped. Heart pounding, she stared at the perfect image.

The gold and lapis lazuli scrollwork, including the central chinoiserie hanging basket motif and delicate eagle's wings on the box, was just as her grandfather had described it. Set on a bed of blue silk, the box stood on its own fragile but exquisitely designed gold pedestal. Both box and pedestal seemed to have been kept in perfect condition in the decades since Giovanni had parted with it.

When she managed to peel her gaze away from the picture, she read the single line beneath it and froze. The reason she hadn't been able to locate the box earlier was because the late queen, Rahim's mother, had kept the box in her bedroom.

The bedroom now used by the current sheikh.

Allegra closed the book with a thump, her body growing numb as reality slid like an insidious fog over her. Until that moment, she hadn't wanted to entertain the thought that she would truly be returning home empty-handed. She'd even toyed with the idea of finding the box herself and getting Rahim to reconsider his position in the morning, with the benefit of time and a little clarity.

From his earlier attitude, it was clear the priceless objects his mother had loved didn't mean as much to him. They were merely flimsy things he'd grown up with. Surely, he wouldn't be as bullheaded in the morning at the thought of parting with one of them?

Shaking her head, she stood a final time and walked out of the office.

The aide waited outside as promised, and walked her to her suite, where Nura greeted her with her usual effervescence. After apologising for keeping her up past midnight, Allegra dismissed her, undressed and pulled on her negligee. She was brushing her hair out when her mobile phone lit up with a voicemail message icon. Dropping the brush, she picked it up and accessed her calls. The Long Island code displayed sent a cold wave of dread through her.

Willing her hands not to shake, she dialled home.

'Miss Allegra, thank God!' Alma exclaimed.

Her grip tightened on the handset until her bones creaked painfully. 'What's happened? Is Grandfather okay?' she demanded.

'Oh, yes. I'm sorry, *piccolina*, I didn't mean to scare you. He's having a better day today, and has been making a bunch of calls all morning. He tried to call you a few times, and you know how he frets when he can't reach any of you.'

Allegra sagged onto the bed in relief, and cursed herself for not taking her phone with her to the banquet. 'Can I talk to him?'

'*Sì*, of course. Hold on.'

Allegra squeezed her eyes shut, dismay at the news she was about to deliver eating her alive.

'Allegra *mia*?' her grandfather greeted her, his voice much stronger than it'd been a few days ago.

'Yes, I'm here, Grandfather.'

'Where exactly is *here*? You've had an old man climbing the walls with worry,' he admonished.

'I'm still in Dar-Aman. I'm sorry, I was at dinner and I didn't bring my phone with me. I…I was going to call you when I got back to New York tomorrow.'

'With good news, yes?' Naked hope pulsed in Giovanni's voice.

Allegra's throat clogged with shame and sorrow. 'Grandfather…' She stopped, unable to find the words that would break his heart.

'I spoke to Matteo an hour ago. He had good news for me regarding the necklace I sent him to find.'

Her heart lurched, and she forced a swallow before she could speak. 'I'm glad, but I couldn't…I don't think I'll be able to retrieve the box for you.'

Heavy silence greeted her confession, broken once by her grandfather's deep, ragged exhalation. 'Was it not there?' he asked, his voice bleak with disappointment.

'It was…it's here. But Rahim…the sheikh, is refusing to part with it.'

Giovanni exhaled again. 'I'm not surprised. It was his mother's treasured possession and must hold sentimental value for him. But… Allegra *mia*, my need is greater, and I've reached a point in this life when I can afford to be a little selfish about my needs.' The confession was hushed, his voice now whispery with desperation. 'If you have seen it, if it's within your grasp, then don't fail me, *ragazza mia*. *Per favore.*' The raw, anguished plea held a note so viscerally harrowing Allegra's eyes prickled.

'This isn't just a box to you, is it, Grandfather?' It couldn't be, not when the thought of not having it back was breaking his heart.

'No, it's not,' he confirmed. When he didn't elaborate, Allegra blinked back her tears and forced strength into her voice.

'I'll bring it back, Nonno. I promise.'

Giovanni exhaled shakily. *'Ti amo, nipotina.'*

Allegra pressed the end button. She knew what she had to do, but didn't allow herself to think beyond her next breath, her next step.

Catching up the wrap she'd dropped on the curved window seat earlier, she tugged it over her negligee and hurried to the door.

The hallway was silent, half of the lamps turned off. The double doors Nura had told her about loomed ominously before her. Fuelled by adrenaline and the promise not to fail again, she grasped the ornate golden handles.

A part of her had feared the doors would be locked. After all, wasn't that how harems worked? Or did Rahim allow whatever woman wanted him to just sail through the doors and into his bedchamber at their whim?

The thought brought acid distaste to her mouth, but not enough to stop her from walking through the doors and shutting them behind her. The hallway snaked into semi-darkness, with a single Tiffany lamp burning on a delicately balanced console table a dozen feet away. Holding her breath, Allegra followed the run of Persian rug, her footsteps muffled by the thick carpet. In the curve of the hallway, she stopped. Heart hammering, she took in the twin Moroccan lanterned lamps bracing either side of giant carved doors.

She didn't need a sign or plaque to tell her those were the doors that led to Rahim's chamber. The heat flooding her veins and the quickening of her blood was evidence enough. But if that wasn't enough, as she forced herself to move closer, his lingering scent curled around her senses. Her nostrils quivered, along with every screeching nerve ending in her body.

Desperately pushing the sensations away, she raised her hand and knocked lightly. She suppressed the half-formed plan bubbling at the edge of her mind and waited. After a full minute, she tried again, then pressed her ear to the door. Fighting not to give in to the voice screaming at her to reconsider what she was doing, she opened the door, again surprised when it gave way.

The living room was vast and probably as breathtaking as the rest of the dreamlike palace, but Allegra was too preoccupied with blocking out the many and varied consequences of being caught to appreciate its beauty. Instead she searched frantically, hoping against hope that the cabinet containing the trinket box had been moved from the bedroom to the living room.

When that optimism was dashed, she hurried, dry-mouthed, through the Moorish arch that led into another room.

Her blood pounding loud enough to drown out every single sound, Allegra entered Rahim's bedroom and stopped. Beneath her bare feet, the softest carpet cushioned her soles, making her toes curl for a delicious second before the sheer visual heaven of her surroundings flattened her.

Although she'd expected it to be grand and opulent beyond her wildest imagination, the sight of Rahim's bedroom made her jaw drop. Every imaginable luxury had been lavished on the room, from the magnificent chandelier from which the stunning frescoes etched into the ceiling seemed to flow from, to the solid gold framed mirrors and paintings positioned around the room.

But it was the sight and position of Rahim's bed that made her eyes widen. Set on four solid pillars, the bed was suspended halfway to the soaring ceiling, with twin curving staircases leading to it from the middle of the cavernous room. Around the heavy cream silk framing the giant four-poster, multipillowed bed, wrought-iron railings, painted a matching gold and white, had been erected. And the headboard, more than twice the size of her own, was even more enthralling, the sheer magnificence of the erotic artwork holding her captive for endless seconds.

Imagining Rahim and his hard, lean body spread out on that bed, heat powered through her, freeing her from her stupor. Dragging her gaze away from the decadent sight, Allegra gulped in air before she snatched back her focus.

Her frantic gaze scoured the endless displays dotted around the room until she found the Louis XIV cabinet she'd seen in the coffee table book. Tightening her hold on her wrap, she sped across the carpeted floor to the display.

Her grandfather's box sat in the middle of the top shelf,

a tiny spotlight showing off the superb craftsmanship and utterly dazzling ornament to full effect. It was beautiful beyond belief, and for the first time since he'd asked her to retrieve it, Allegra accepted how special the box was.

Heart in her throat, she took a step closer to the cabinet, then whirled around with a gasp at the sound of a door sliding shut behind her.

Rahim entered the room and every atom in Allegra's body screamed alive. First with dread. Then with a fiery excitement so strong she wondered whether she'd turn to char by the time the man who was rubbing his hair with a towel, and hadn't yet seen her, realised she'd violated his privacy.

Rahim lowered the towel a second later, then froze. Shock flared through his eyes, before the hazel depths darkened. Narrow-eyed, he stalked across the bedroom floor, his gaze pinned like lasers on her.

With each step, Allegra cautioned herself not to look at his body. To instead think of a plausible explanation as to why she was here, in the middle of the night, dressed as flimsily as she was.

By his fourth step, she'd lost the battle. Her eyes devoured the wide, lean expanse of his shoulders, and the hard, washboard stomach. Against the stark white towel knotted carelessly at his waist, his dark olive skin glowed with mouth-watering vibrancy, his skin so gloriously sleek her fingers burned to touch. Desire dredged through her belly and her mouth flooded with acute hunger as he neared and she saw the droplets of water clinging to his skin.

He was beautiful beyond words; from the ink-black damp hair to the powerful legs eating up the distance between them, Rahim Al-Hadi was a panther-like specimen of male beauty, and she accepted in that moment that she couldn't hold that against him. Not when every inch of her wanted to be plastered to every inch of him. Long and hard and in every imaginable position possible.

'Allegra,' he breathed her name, his voice heavy with an emotion she couldn't name, but which echoed all the way through her body. 'I'm not sure whether to applaud you for your reckless daring, or chastise you for your foolishness in coming here.'

The deep growl in his voice made the secret place between her thighs throb urgently. Chagrined, she wondered how she could react like this to his voice alone, even as her breasts tingled, her nipples turning to hard peaks at the blatant hunger in his face.

'I hope you don't mind, but I couldn't sleep, not without coming here to...' She trailed off uselessly as he shifted the towel from his neck and flung it away. In her bare feet, she was eye level with his pecs, and with the absence of the towel, his flat, brown nipples were displayed in perfect, round discs.

'Coming here to...?' he echoed mockingly.

She blinked. Tried to breathe.

God. Think, Allegra!

'I...I wasn't happy with the way we left things. I wanted to make amends.'

Rahim took another dangerous step closer, and she caught the faint smell of chlorine mingled with an earthier scent of warm, male skin. A visual image of him, swimming naked, surged up to collide with all the X-rated images speeding through her brain.

'And how exactly do you wish to make amends?'

For as long as she lived, Allegra doubted she would be able to explain the sensation that overtook her in that moment. Perhaps she had been seeking a connection to something...or someone...all along without realising it. Certainly, the feeling of being adrift, of being alone since she lost her mother countless years ago, had been a pain waiting to rear up and stab her in her weakest moments. It wasn't a feeling she freely expressed, because she knew her sisters and brothers viewed their often volatile mother differently, that they wouldn't welcome Allegra's lonely sentiment. Nor would she want to remind them of how she'd personally failed them when it came to providing the stability they'd needed when it'd most counted.

Whatever she was suppressing, the moment her hand connected with the naked flesh of Rahim's torso, a deep, visceral emotion moved through her that made her soul sigh in relief and surrender.

Warm and alive and vitally intoxicating, she could no more stop touching him, exploring him, than she could stop breathing.

Sleek muscle clenched beneath her touch, followed by a sharp intake of breath.

When she managed to pull her gaze from the expanse of skin heating her fingers, she glanced up to see eyes lit with a voracious fire that threatened to consume her. Knowing he wanted her as much as she wanted him lent Allegra the strength to make the next, completely insane, but almost inevitable, move.

Because in that moment, she couldn't *not* kiss the sensual lips that were parted hungrily. Nor could she *not* wrap her hand around his thick neck and draw herself up. Up to taste the exotic decadence of his mouth. Up to lose herself in the fever infusing her blood.

His lips were warm, drug-like in their complete intoxication of her senses and firm in their demand. They clung to hers, allowed her to explore… He even let her pull away for a second when the wonder of it overwhelmed her. Eyes glued to one another, their breaths mingled as he waited, for what, Allegra couldn't tell.

But with the inevitability of a diver jumping from a plane, she surged up for another taste. And in the space of

a heartbeat, Rahim was devouring her. Strong, corded arms
lashed her body to his, his grip so tight she could barely
breathe. Not that breathing was uppermost in her mind. No,
the tongue sliding against hers, driving her senses wild,
was more an urgent need. One she couldn't get enough of
no matter how much she strained against him.

A moan slipped free, which triggered an answering
groan from Rahim. Her fingers traced his neck, gloried in
the pulse hammering at his throat, before spiking into his
damp hair. Against her belly, the thin covering of his towel
did nothing to disguise the surging evidence of his arousal.

Wetness pooling between her thighs, singeing her with
even greater need, she strained closer. Then almost cried
out in despair when Rahim gripped her waist and set her
away from him.

Breaths panting, they stared at each other. Allegra had
no words to describe the state she was in, so she gazed
mutely at him, hoping against hope that he wasn't about
to send her away. The very thought made the fingers she'd
clenched in his hair tighten.

'This is how you want to make amends?' he enquired,
his voice gravel-hoarse with arousal. 'Think carefully before you answer, *habibi*. Because once you answer in the
affirmative, once I have you in my bed, there will be no
going back.'

She wanted to tell him she knew she'd already burned
bridges where he was concerned. From the moment they'd
touched, she'd known Rahim Al-Hadi had inexplicable
power over her. Allegra knew it was why she'd reacted so
uncharacteristically strongly to him. Whether she wanted
him to matter or not, Rahim spoke to a need in her soul
she couldn't deny.

And right here, right now, she didn't want to.

'Yes,' she whispered. Then in a stronger voice because
her very soul demanded it, she repeated, 'Yes, I want this.'

CHAPTER SEVEN

RAHIM STARED INTO Allegra's face, her beauty momentarily blinding him to the reality that he needed to stop…walk away before things escalated out of control. They were already a light year from how he'd expected things to go when he'd entered his bedroom and found her here.

Having resigned himself to seeing the last of her in his study, and having taken out the brunt of his anger at her duplicity in an hour-long pounding in his private swimming pool, finding her scantily clad and looking guilty as hell had been a shock.

Hard on the heels of shock had been disappointment—that she was no better than any of the females he'd availed himself of in his past life who always wanted something from him—followed closely by the resurgence of anger. That he'd read her motives for coming to Dar-Aman so wrong. That she was so set on securing material assets that she was unwilling to consider offering the vital assistance he needed for his people.

But as Rahim had stood there debating whether to throw her out or go one better and call security, other, more urgent needs had taken over. He wasn't ashamed to admit those needs, after that kiss that threatened to blow his mind, now reigned supreme.

However, he knew her motives weren't as altruistic as she pretended, so he forced himself to slow down, to give her a chance to redeem herself, even as his fingers dug into her waist to hold her in place, and every cell in his body screamed at him to take what she offered, gorge on the feast she'd laid at his feet.

'Are you sure?'

She let out a laugh, probably designed to entice. Instead the clear nervousness in the sound curled around a hard kernel of his remaining resolve, melting it to nothing. Then her hand unclenched from his hair and slid along his stubbled jaw. When her shaky fingers traced his lower lip, Rahim groaned low and deep.

'Before I came here, I was known for saying what I mean and meaning what I said.' She laughed again, the sound easier, if a little hungrier than before. 'I haven't demonstrated it as well as I should, but yes, I'm sure.' The last bit was whispered, her blue eyes turning several shades darker as her gaze locked on his lips.

Knowing she wanted his kiss, and much more, lit pure fire in Rahim's veins. He caught her roving finger into his mouth and suckled hard. Her eyes widened. For a second, he wondered about her sexual experience, then lost himself in the expression of wonder on her face as her gaze locked on what he was doing to her finger. Testing her further, he licked the tip, and she gasped.

Desire pounded through him as the many ways he could have her flared across his senses. Reaching for the wrap hiding her from him, he ripped it away.

Her negligee was a silk-and-lace concoction, delicate enough to tear at the slightest exertion. The temptation to do just that was strong, but Rahim exercised restraint. Anger and disappointment were no longer overriding emotions— he would triumph in finding a way out of his predicament, he always did—but they remained buried beneath more urgent, earthier needs. Needs so voracious he forced himself to pause a beat as her heaving breasts straining against her thin silk sent renewed hunger roaring through him.

Catching her beneath her hips, he strode quickly to the fireplace set beneath the pillared elevation of his bed. Before the flickering flames dancing between the coals, he laid her down on soft cashmere rugs and sat back on his heels.

The flames reflected off her glowing skin a few shades lighter than his own but exhibiting her Latin ancestry.

Slowly, he traced the sweet curve of her jaw, to the pulse hammering at her throat. She shivered and squirmed, her movements innocently seductive as she stared up at him.

For a long moment, Rahim didn't move, arrested as he was by her.

'Please…'

'Shh, let me enjoy you for a moment, for you are an exquisite sight to behold.' The clear outline of her nipples drew his touch and he circled the bud with his finger, drawing an urgent cry from her that echoed deep within him.

Sliding the straps from her shoulders, he bared her to him. 'Exquisite,' he repeated.

Bracing himself on his elbows, Rahim drew one velvety tip into his mouth. Her groan was so intoxicating he repeated the act, then again on her other breast.

'Oh, Rahim,' she choked out.

'You like that?'

Her nostrils quivered delicately as she inhaled. 'Yes,' she breathed.

'You want more?' he demanded, a keen desire to see her completely undone overcoming him.

At her eager nod, he flicked his tongue against her, then caught the wet, pebbled flesh between his teeth. Her nails scored his shoulders and she arched her back.

Rahim clawed at his fraying control, warning himself that this was just a means of sating his lust. Of taking what she was freely offering and perhaps teaching her a lesson in the process. There was no need for this to be something else, something alien that scrabbled at a place he'd sealed off a long time ago. A place that reeked of loneliness and neglect. A place that reminded him too much of his adolescent years.

He wasn't lonely. Or desperate for the connection that had been missing in his life for longer than he cared to recall. He'd learned to do without it. He'd found other, more fruitful ways to find the closure that had eluded him. By taking his rightful place on the throne as all Al-Hadis had done in the past, and vowing to care for his people, he'd sealed off that part of himself that wanted closure.

He didn't need closure if he intended to take up the mantle destiny had handed him.

He certainly didn't *need* the warm, vibrant woman beneath him, not even for one single night the way his senses were tricking him into believing. This would be a brief, if thoroughly pleasurable, coupling before he sent her on her way.

That was all it would ever be.

'Rahim?' Her sultry voice centred his attention back on her and he happily abandoned his unsettling thoughts.

'Yes, *habibi*? Tell me what you want.'

Her back arched higher, seeking his attention. 'More, please?'

Squeezing the perfect globes, he lowered his head. 'It'll be my pleasure.'

Allegra almost cried in relief when his mouth closed over her again. For a moment, she'd feared he would stop. Certainly the bleakness that had clouded his eyes and stolen his focus had sent a cold shiver through her, the brief glimpse of pain momentarily stopping her desire in its tracks.

Curiously, in that moment, she hadn't felt a loss at his lack of attention. Watching emotions she recognised in herself flit over his face had evoked a surprising affinity. One she'd quickly banished because she knew in her deepest heart that Rahim wouldn't welcome such a connection.

Lust and sex were more acceptable to him.

And with the touch of his lips, everything besides the feverish sensations firing up her body melted away. Including the cautionary voice that questioned what on earth she was doing.

She was living. She was providing her soul with much-needed sustenance even she hadn't known was missing until she'd touched Rahim. She was absolutely certain this would be a one-time thing, so she staunched the voice and gave herself over completely to the bliss rampaging through her. Dug her nails deeper into his shoulders, arched her back higher and vocalised her groans.

He tugged on her negligee, his movements a touch rougher than they had been a moment ago. Allegra watched the firelight dance over his sculpted features as he pulled down her garment and flung it away. Her panties quickly followed.

Being naked with a man for the first time in a very long time drew a well of self-consciousness within her. And the way Rahim's gaze scoured her, leaving no inch untouched, made her squirm harder, his scrutiny almost a living thing on her skin.

Unconsciously, her arms started to move to cover herself. He captured them and pinned them down beside her hips. 'Don't deny me, Allegra. Stay,' he commanded gutturally. 'Let me look and have my fill.'

He let go of her, staggered away for a handful of seconds and returned with a condom. Dropping to his knees, he framed her body with his hands. From neck to thigh, he caressed her while his eyes devoured her. By the time he hooked his hands behind her knees and parted her, Allegra had forgotten what it felt like to breathe. Each caress pushed her higher on a plane of pure heart-pounding de-sire, where plea-filled words crowded her brain, ready to fall should he keep her waiting a moment longer.

As if he knew the depth of her desperation, he crashed forward, took her mouth in another voracious kiss. Their tongues duelled, their mouths melding in bruising kiss after bruising kiss, until with a groan he yanked his towel free, donned the protection and positioned himself be-tween her thighs.

With one hand locked in her hair, he tilted her head up. 'Look at me.' Lust throbbed in his voice, but there was also a tinge of anger.

And when she lifted lust-drugged eyes to his, she wit-nessed a sliver of cruelty in there. Not enough to stop her though. She exhaled as she felt him, solid and strong, against her core. 'Open wider for me.'

She complied with a helpless groan, then whimpered when he still hesitated. 'Rahim, please.'

A fevered flush flared across his cheekbones, a sheen of sweat coating his upper lip as he gritted out, 'Tell me again that this is what you want.'

Allegra angled her hips, desperately bringing herself closer to the promise of oblivion. 'Yes. I want you, please. Take me— *Oh!*'

Rahim drove into her, his penetration sure and powerful and complete enough to drive her breath from her lungs. On the heels of his uncompromising possession came a surge of pleasure so amazing Allegra could only stare up at him in wonder.

Then he moved.

Hot, guttural Dar-Amanian words fell from his lips and a visible shudder shook his frame as he slammed back in, then held himself deep and solid inside her.

'Heaven above, you feel incredible,' he groaned when he moved again.

Allegra couldn't find words, so she held on tight as he increased his scorching rhythm, taking her with a mastery that heaped pleasure on top of pleasure with each thrust. Somewhere along the line, he released his grip on her hair, and transferred his hold to her hip. Holding her steady, he took her higher, deeper still, all the while kissing her, and muttering indecipherable words against her skin when he drew away.

The raw beauty of the act seared her soul, and when the pressure got too much, tears filled her eyes.

'Rahim…' Allegra didn't know what she wanted. All she knew was that the feeling inside her was too much to contain. Sliding her hands up his jaw to his cheeks, she cradled his face in her hands, stared deep into his eyes as her world exploded into flames and ecstasy buffeted her in relentless waves.

His own scorching release followed swiftly on the heels of hers. Allegra watched in awe as he threw back his arrogant head, gave a hoarse cry before a series of deep shudders raked his frame. He collapsed on top of her, and their breaths mingled as their racing hearts began to calm.

Minutes passed by before Rahim rose on one elbow and brushed her hair away from her face. Although she'd closed her eyes at some point, Allegra felt his keen scrutiny. But she wasn't prepared for the words that fell like barbs from his lips.

'If this is how you make amends, then I'm all for it.'

She stiffened, her heart clenching with hurt despite the knowledge that she'd brought his response on herself. Opening her eyes, she met fierce, hazel ones. 'You could at least wait until I'm dressed before you hurl the insults,' she breathed.

'Insults? I thought you were all for speaking freely and honestly? I in turn meant what I just said. Give me another taste of your body and you can consider your apology accepted and your slate wiped clean,' he said. 'That is if that was what you really came here for?' A cynical smile touched his lips, but it was replaced a moment later by male appreciation as he transferred his gaze from her face to her body, then back again.

She lowered her gaze, unable to withstand the challenge and suspicion in his eyes. Her insides clenched in shame at how utterly she'd let herself down since stepping foot in Dar-Aman.

'It was…but my gesture was finite.' She started to move away, but he caught her arm and held her still.

'Where do you think you're going?'

'Back to my room, of course.'

One finger caught her beneath her chin and compelled her gaze to his. Hunger, wilder than before, blazed in his eyes. 'I told you I intended to have my fill. I've barely started, Allegra. You're going nowhere until I'm done with you.'

The shameless part of her that craved what he offered melted with a swiftness that robbed her of breath. She scrambled to gather a semblance of thought as his head lowered dangerously towards hers. 'I have no intention of being your plaything, Rahim. I'll leave that to the women in your harem.'

He looked surprised for a moment before a low laugh spilled from his lips. 'I stopped having playthings the moment I hit puberty, *habibi*.'

The absence of denial of his harem set a different blaze in her belly that made her squirm to get away from him. 'Whatever. I'm still leaving in the morning.'

'And I have no intention of stopping you,' he parried with arrogant ease, as if she was one of the many ornaments in his palace to be taken or left at his whim. 'But there are many hours between now and morning and I intend to fill them all.'

Allegra told herself she should be thankful that Rahim had proved her right in one aspect—he was a playboy who bedded and discarded women as frequently as he changed his regal clothes. She told herself she ought to have more self-respect, leave while the absurd feelings of hurt and bewildering anger weren't choking her.

But then his hand slid down her belly to the place that still throbbed hard and mercilessly from his possession. A weak, helpless moan escaped her before she could kill it.

Even to her own ears, the sound of surrender was enough to halt her in her tracks.

She would never see Rahim Al-Hadi again. He was the very epitome of a no-strings-attached one-night stand. Hell, by this time tomorrow, he'd have forgotten she existed.

Why couldn't she do the same? Use him as he was using her?

Because that's not who you are...

'Stay with me, Allegra,' he demanded harshly.

Allegra's disturbing thoughts melted as his fingers curled, expertly teasing her heated flesh. She tried to shake her head but he only increased his exquisite torture. Her body, having had a taste of what pleasures were in store for it, completely betrayed her, undulating to his command as bliss overtook her.

'Stay with me,' he demanded again his tone gentler. His head dipped and he caught her nipple in his mouth. His tongue swirled around the bud before he pulled it deep into his mouth.

With a deep groan, Allegra gasped, 'Yes.'

At some point, he carried her from the fireplace, up the stairs to his bed. In between intoxicating bouts of love-making, Allegra took in the view from her lofty position, her senses drowning in the wonder of floating on a bed of dreams.

But dream turned into nightmare somewhere around dawn when she jerked awake, the ephemeral thoughts that had been niggling at the edge of her brain finally sending her on a frantic search. Hands shaking, she located the condom. The *ripped* condom which she hadn't thought twice about when she'd grasped Rahim in a particularly heated moment but which her subconscious must have documented.

Waves of ice drenching her, she slid from her bed and stood with her heart thudding dully. Thoughts of the possible consequences slammed through her mind, each worse case more frightening than the last. She took deep, steady breaths, forcing herself not to panic. She was on the pill, one with high levels of success. And that last, lust-inflamed move, she concluded, face flaming hotter, had been right before their final release. Her fears abated slightly as she confirmed that her pill dosage was right on track.

It had to be.

She was nowhere near equipped to assume the huge responsibility of caring for a child.

Her track record was woefully lacking to even begin to contemplate motherhood.

And really, would the odds be so cruelly stacked against her for seeking one moment of passion?

But it hadn't been just the once...

Rahim had stayed true to his word. His hunger hadn't abated until the first streaks of an orange sunrise tinged grey skies. Her body ached in places thoroughly alien to her and, with each breath, she felt the residual power of his possession.

Allegra knew that if it hadn't been for her subconscious nudging her to acknowledge her folly, she would be as dead to the world as Rahim was now. Her breath caught anew as she stared down at him.

In sleep, he was a little less overpowering, but every bit

as magnificent. With the sheets tangled around his waist and one arm thrown over his head, his incredible body was on display, reminding her just how hungry *she'd* been in turn. How hungry she *still* was. The force of that need had her taking a step back. When her back touched the cold railing, she suppressed a gasp.

She was naked in the bedchamber of a man she hadn't met this time yesterday. A man who was only supposed to have been a means to an end. An end she'd failed woefully at achieving.

Far from the woman she'd taken pride in believing herself to be once she'd acknowledged her basic flaws, Allegra felt the humiliating burn of deep shame and she hurried silently down the stairs to the lower floor of Rahim's chamber. Each stealthy breath she took hammered home her spectacular failure.

Ruthlessly she locked her thoughts down to be dealt with when she was far away from Dar-Aman. It was either that or lose her mind along with everything she'd thrown under the bus of her weakness. Slipping her wrinkled negligee over her head, she crossed to where Rahim had dropped her wrap earlier. As she straightened, her gaze fell on the Fabergé box.

Don't fail me, ragazza mia.

Her grandfather's words resonated loudly in her head, as if he stood next to her. Hopeless tears filled her eyes. She plugged the sob that threatened with her fist and took a step back from the cabinet.

She couldn't.

She *wouldn't*.

But hadn't she lost everything she deemed worthy tonight? She'd come into Rahim's room with the intention of finding *some* way of taking possession of the box. When he'd caught her red-handed, she'd lied and thrown herself at him to cover her subterfuge.

Her integrity was already in shreds. But did that warrant adding *stealing* to her sins?

She shook her head as another sob rose. She'd failed her family in so many ways. Adding another failure... returning home to her grandfather empty-handed... The thought tore at her heart.

Hands shaking, she slid back the cabinet glass and reached for the box. Shrugging her wrap off her shoulders, she wrapped the priceless ornament in it and slowly turned.

With one last quick glance up to where Rahim lay sleeping, she slipped out as quietly as she'd entered.

But even as her feet carried her back to her suite, and she hurried through packing her suitcase and reassuring a bewildered Nura that she would much prefer a taxi to the airport over a palace driver, Allegra was certain the stain on her soul would never be erased.

The stain deepened even as she sent silent thanks to the media who'd widely documented her visit with Rahim. As a guest of His Royal Highness, she was informed with deference by the airport officials; she didn't need to go through customs. Allegra cringed with shame as she was escorted into her first-class seat on the commercial jet.

Nevertheless, she cradled her grandfather's Lost Mistress throughout the flight, unwilling to let it out of her sight.

The tiny voice that mocked that she did so because the box also signified the only part of Rahim she would ever encounter again in this lifetime, she harshly ignored.

CHAPTER EIGHT

Two months later

ALLEGRA HEARD THE slow footsteps and the added click of the walking stick and summoned a smile as her grandfather walked into the sunroom.

Situated on the east wing of the Long Island villa, the shaded coolness of the room was what Giovanni favoured these days, although he spent an hour on his favourite terrace in the mornings, before the mid-July heat became too unbearable.

She turned in her seat as the footsteps halted. '*Ragazza*, I didn't hear you come in.'

'I didn't want to disturb you. Alma said you were resting.'

He waved an impatient hand. 'She's very liberal with her guard dog duties, that one. I was merely cataloguing a few things in my study after lunch. She could've let me know you were here at any time,' he grumbled.

Allegra knew it was more than just cataloguing. Ever since she'd returned the Fabergé box to her grandfather, he'd kept it in his study, alongside a necklace whose origin was unknown to her. She knew from the housekeeper that Giovanni had been spending hours in his study with the two pieces lately. 'It doesn't matter. You're here now. It's good to see you up.'

'I have my good days and bad days. Today is a good

day.' Her grandfather walked forward, his stride a little slow, but his colour much better than it'd been back in May.

Before he'd sent her to Dar-Aman.

Before her life had changed forever.

The mingled feelings of awe, fear and dread that spiralled through her every time she thought of the secret she carried ate away at her smile. Dragging it back, she met her grandfather halfway and kissed him on both cheeks.

When she drew back, she met his frank gaze, praying he wouldn't comment on her sallow complexion or the weight she'd lost.

'Something's wrong, Allegra *mia*,' he said, dashing her hopes. When she opened her mouth, he shook his head. 'Don't bother denying it. You're good at hiding things but you forget that you are my blood, my first granddaughter. Ever since you were a child you cared for everyone else around you. That special trait is why I chose you to head my foundation. You care—a little too much, some might say—but you don't care enough about yourself.'

Allegra couldn't help the bitterness in her voice. 'I disagree. I don't think my caring was enough.'

Giovanni shuffled to the wide armchair and sank heavily into it. After propping his cane next to the chair, he turned his frown on her. 'Being exceptionally hard on yourself has always been your problem.'

'One of many, I'm sure.'

His frown deepened. 'My dear, what's happened to resurrect these self-doubting ghosts? I thought you'd put them behind you years ago? Did something happen during your little trip?'

Allegra started in surprise, then shook her head. 'I... It's nothing I can't handle.'

'So there *is* something?' her grandfather probed.

Allegra had to ball her fist to keep from sliding her hand over her stomach. She'd caught herself making that uncon-

scious gesture a lot lately, once she'd finished the book
that tracked the growth of her baby in minute detail. Her
baby might be the size of a bean, but the very idea that life
grew inside her was a phenomenon she hadn't quite come
to terms with six weeks after discovering that, against all
odds, she carried Rahim Al-Hadi's child in her womb.

'Allegra?'

Everything inside her wanted to spill her secret. But
how could she admit to carrying such a responsibility when
she didn't feel worthy of it?

'I have a lot on my plate, that's all. The women's rights
conference in Geneva's coming up and preparations are
frantic as usual. You know how making speeches turns
me into a blubbering wreck.' She laughed, and her grandfather cracked a smile, but she saw the lingering specula-
tion in his shrewd eyes.

'Bianca is assisting you with it, right?'

Allegra nodded, relieved her grandfather had cho-
sen not to pursue the subject. 'She's handling publicity
through Lucia PR, but the keynote speech is my responsibility.' A responsibility she'd barely given her full attention to since the severe bouts of morning sickness had hit
exactly two weeks after she'd confirmed her pregnancy.
It was hard enough to concentrate when thoughts of the
many ways she could screw up her child's life multiplied
with each waking hour that passed. Add the terrifying
thought of how and when she'd break the news to Rahim,
and what his reaction would be, and the task of putting
together a rousing speech on empowering women fled
from her mind.

With the conference a short seven days away, she'd finally given in and solicited her sister's help. Bianca had
jumped at the chance to add the Di Sione Foundation to
her growing high-profile clients and had taken charge of
publicising the event.

Now all Allegra had to do was write the speech. And come up with a plan for the future of the child growing inside her.

She felt the blood drain from her face as nausea rose in her belly. Swallowing hard, she looked up to find Giovanni staring intently at her. 'It'll be fine, I'm sure.'

He nodded, but his eyes remained serious. '*Sì*, it will be. You've never failed in anything you've undertaken, *nipotina*. You will overcome this too. I have faith in you.'

Allegra tried selfishly to hold on to those words, despite knowing that her grandfather hadn't been in possession of all the facts when he'd made the statement. She hadn't failed in retrieving his box because she'd stolen it, and shattered any chance of being seen as anything but a common thief in Rahim's eyes.

By the time she packed her bags to head to Geneva, her grandfather's reassuring words had dwindled to nothing, annihilated by looming fear and doubt that warned her she was condemning her child to a life of uncertainty and insecurity.

How could she offer her child love when her own experience with it had been a twisted version, often fuelled by bouts of heartbroken wailing on her mother's part, and volatile cocktails of drugs and booze with a healthy bout of rage thrown in from her father?

How could she trust herself to do the right thing for her child when more than once she'd feared the blood that ran through her was tainted somehow? Alessandro, her oldest brother, had buried himself in the family business from very early on, and her twin brothers had borne all the hallmarks of turning into their father, despite her grandfather's repeated intervention. As much as it broke her heart to admit it, her failure to adequately sustain her family when they'd needed her most had left flaws entrenched too deep to ever make them whole.

But…the alternative was inconceivable.

She laid her hand over her still-flat stomach, and for the first time, Allegra's heart leapt, not with fear, but with a tiny geyser of joy. She held on to it through another bout of morning sickness once she got to her hotel. Then through the hours of polishing her speech in preparation for the conference the next day.

It had gone ten p.m. by the time she saved the finalised version on her laptop and called to check on her grandfather. About to turn in, she frowned as her phone buzzed.

Reading the message, she groaned and slid back out of bed.

She opened the door to her sister, eyeing Bianca's fresh-as-a-daisy look with a tiny bout of envy. In a monochrome dress suit and stylish platform shoes, she looked ready to powwow her way through a power meeting, not wind down for the night.

'Wow, you look like hell run over by a truck.'

'Oh, thanks.' Allegra shut the door and leaned against it with her arms folded.

Bianca grinned, the confidence she radiated so effortlessly lending her a vivacity that turned heads wherever she went. It was the reason she'd become a success in the public relations industry so quickly. 'Can I order room service? I'm starving!'

'And I need to sleep. Don't you have your own suite?'

One of the reasons Bianca remained the sibling she was closest to was because of their similar tastes in a broad range of things, including food. But since Allegra couldn't stomach foods she'd once loved, she couldn't risk Bianca guessing her state if she ordered the same turkey sandwich that had disagreed with Allegra earlier this evening.

'I do, but I wanted to go over a few things with you before things got crazy in the morning. So here I am, killing two birds blah-blah-blah.'

Allegra regarded her sister with one sceptical eyebrow raised.

After a minute, Bianca shrugged. 'Okay, fine. The last-minute stuff with the conference can wait.'

'But?' Allegra prompted.

'*But* I spoke to Grandfather half an hour ago. He sounded worried about you. Everything okay? Seriously, you don't look great. And you've lost weight since I last saw you.'

Allegra waved her sister away, moving from the door and from Bianca's direct gaze, which was so reminiscent of her grandfather's. When her sister followed her into the living room, Allegra suppressed a weary sigh.

'I'm fine. I ate something that didn't agree with me earlier, that's all.' That much was true. The cold turkey sandwich had stayed in her stomach less than five minutes before it'd come straight back out.

'That would explain how you look now, but it doesn't explain the weight loss.'

Striding to the fridge, Allegra took out a bottle of water, and toyed with it. 'Enough with the third degree. Did you need something else besides the desire to bug me?'

Bianca pursed her lips, then strode over to face Allegra across the tiny drinks bar in the living room. 'Grandfather asked to see me last week,' she blurted.

Thinking her sister was intent on getting to the bottom of her weight loss, Allegra tensed. 'And?'

'He asked me to find something for him.'

Allegra's relief was overlaid with surprise. 'What?'

'A bracelet. He sold it years ago, but now he wants it back…' Her voice trailed off and then she sucked in a quick breath. 'Matteo was asked to find something too, wasn't he?'

Allegra nodded. 'A necklace. Grandfather sent me to find something as well.'

Her sister's eyes widened. 'Really? Did you find it?'

'Yes, it was a box, a Fabergé.'

Bianca's eyes grew wider. 'You think they're all connected somehow?'

'I don't know. He wasn't very forthcoming when I asked.'

'Same here.' She frowned. 'Allegra, these are expensive pieces. And didn't Grandfather say he landed on Ellis Island with just the clothes on his back?' Her expression grew wistful. 'Maybe they belonged to a long-lost love?'

Hearing the longing in her sister's voice, Allegra allowed herself to be pulled into the world of *what if* for the briefest moment. *What if* she had known love, enough to be sure her child would be emotionally secure? *What if* things had gone differently with Rahim, and she hadn't burned every single bridge in sight to the ground.

Sharply rousing herself from her futile musing, she opened the bottle of water and poured it into a glass. After taking a careful sip, she glanced at her sister. 'As far as I know, Grandmother was the only woman Grandfather loved. If there's any more to these items, I'm sure he'll let us know when he's ready.'

Bianca sighed, then grimaced. 'Practical Allegra, party pooper.'

The nickname rubbed her the wrong way, but Allegra kept her composure. After agreeing to meet her in the conference room an hour before it started, Bianca left.

Sliding back in bed, Allegra placed her hand on her stomach. This time the fissure cracked wider, filling her with a warm and protective emotion that made her heart lurch.

From the moment she'd found out, even not knowing which course she would take, she'd safeguarded her baby's physical health. But Allegra knew she couldn't ignore the tougher emotional aspect of her situation. She had to tell Rahim.

If nothing else for the fact that the baby she carried was the heir apparent to a desert kingdom. A kingdom whose ruler, she now knew, had been battling against severe odds to do the right thing for his people.

On her return, Allegra had commissioned a more thorough report on Dar-Aman and confirmed Rahim's claim that things had ground to a halt the moment his mother had died. And in the almost two decades since, Dar-Aman had slipped into devastating decline. But in the past six months the changes Rahim had put into place were staggering. With the economy in free fall, most of the infrastructure rebuilding had been financed by his personal wealth. Contrary to her accusation that he was draining Dar-Aman's resources to line his own pockets, he'd been doing the opposite.

No wonder he'd been livid.

Shifting in bed, Allegra hugged her pillow close and squeezed her eyes shut. She owed Rahim an apology, possibly more than one.

Taking a deep breath she formulated a plan. Her doctor had told her she would start showing in a little over eight weeks. Regardless of her personal feelings about it, she was fast running out of time to keep her secret to herself.

She would find a way to deliver the news to Rahim before Mother Nature did the job for her. She may have thoroughly and completely bungled her own life, but she owed her baby every decent chance to grow up with as much emotional security as she could provide. And that included giving him or her a chance to know both parents.

Allegra woke in a better frame of mind than she had since discovering she was carrying Rahim's baby. She even managed to eat and keep down a whole slice of toast before Bianca knocked on her door at ten.

Together they headed to the vast conference room. As the keynote speaker, her seat was dead centre in the giant amphitheatre. All around her, seats soared to the ceiling, ready to be filled by men and women from all walks of life whose passion for rights for women burned as fiercely as hers.

For the first time in a long while, Allegra felt pride for what she'd accomplished. When her grandfather's words whispered across her mind, she smiled and hugged it closer.

'That's better. You seem almost human this morning,' Bianca quipped.

She laughed. 'As opposed to…?'

'Dead Barbie Walking?'

Allegra rolled her eyes. 'Yeah, right. I've never done anything remotely doll-like in my life, and you know it.'

Bianca smiled. 'True. Your role has always been more of a fairy godmother stroke sister.'

We're not fictional characters, Allegra…I prefer to live in reality, no matter how unpalatable it can be…

The stark words Rahim had uttered blazed across her mind. Would he find the reality of impending fatherhood unpalatable? Ice drenched her at the thought of a rejection she couldn't rule out of her immediate future. As a child she'd bore the brunt of such a rejection from her own father. Was she wise to risk exposing her own child to such a fate?

'Hey, what did I say?' Bianca enquired anxiously.

She shook her head. 'Nothing at all.' Shaking herself free of the dread closing in on her, she plastered yet another fake smile on her face. 'Tell me what I need to do.'

After a brief examination of Allegra's face, her sister shook her head resignedly. 'There are three cameras trained on you. We're broadcasting live, but there's a five-second delay in case anything *extraordinary* happens—please make sure it doesn't or I'll skin you alive. Once you're done, I'll feed the coverage to the smaller news channels and social media, then do the same for the guest speakers. I won't bore you with the smaller details, but I've told your assistant to set aside an hour for you to do a few press junkets after lunch. And that's it. Now go put some colour in those cheeks before everyone arrives.'

Allegra left the stage, conscious of her sister's worry. Praying that she would hold it together for just a while longer, she went into the restroom, sat on the pedestal and concentrated on breathing.

The knock on the stall door sent her surging to her feet. 'Yes?'

'Allegra, are you okay?' Zara asked. 'Your sister sent me to find you. The conference is about to start.'

Startled, she glanced at her watch and realised she'd been in there half an hour. 'Thanks, I'll be right out.'

Rushing out, Allegra washed her hands and reapplied her lipstick. She didn't need extra colour in her cheeks because her mortification had taken care of that.

Striding onto the stage, she offered quick smiles to her fellow speakers as she took her seat. In the time she'd been locked in the restroom the conference room had filled to capacity.

Allegra told herself the intense tingling along her spine was because she was the centre of attention. But as the organiser and first guests took the podium, the sensation escalated from a tingle to shivers of awareness that wouldn't abate.

When her name was announced, Allegra rose on shaky legs and approached the podium. Reaching the lectern she adjusted the mic, and looked up.

Straight into the icily condemning eyes of Rahim Al-Hadi.

CHAPTER NINE

RAHIM STARED AT her from his seat on the front row. He had to hand it to her. Not once did her mask of professionalism slip, despite the tension that seized her body when their eyes met. A pulse of satisfaction went through him at the reaction. To everyone else, she was merely waiting for the applause to die down before she spoke. But Rahim had caught the tiny gasp which had escaped her parted lips and the darkening of her blue eyes before she regained her composure.

Had he received a cold, callous dismissal from her, he wasn't sure that he would've been able to remain seated. The depths of her duplicity notwithstanding, the fact that he hadn't been able to stop thinking about Allegra had been a mild irritation at first but then had grown into an insidious ache that he couldn't seem to get rid of. Rahim hadn't been able to understand it at first. He'd had great sex with countless faceless women, but never had he woken up to a gnawing bewilderment as to why a woman's absence from his bed would disturb him enough to become a problem.

And Allegra had become a problem. Quite apart from helping herself to property that didn't belong to her, her barbs about the state of his kingdom and the women in particular had stuck long after she had stolen away from his bed like the slippery thief she was. Rahim told himself it was the only reason why he'd made the trip to

Geneva. The sexual aspect of their encounter would die down once he'd got rid of the blemish she'd attempted to stain his character with and walked away for good.

He refocused on her face, listened to her impassioned speech about equality and the empowerment of women through the granting of greater rights. The sound of her voice, husky and beautifully cadenced, threatened to cut through the cold rage locked in his chest. Much like had been happening with far too much frequency in the past few weeks, he recalled her heated implorations as he'd trapped her beneath him and scaled new heights of ecstasy with her. Like every rapt member of the audience, he'd been enthralled with her, enough so that as he'd fallen asleep that night two months ago, he toyed with the idea of prolonging their encounter.

Even waking up and discovering the theft, Rahim had been willing to consider letting her keep the box if it meant convincing her to stay in Dar-Aman a little while longer. Discovering her gone, and the piercing ache of disappointment that had followed, had sent an icy premonition down his spine. The reminder of his father's weakness where his mother was concerned and the parallels to what he was willing to let slide because of one woman had been shocking enough to bid Allegra good riddance. But, Rahim thought bitterly, out of sight hadn't meant out of mind.

She paused in her speech, allowing the captive audience to share in her joke. For a brief moment, her eyes slid to his. The shock she hadn't quite been able to hide reflected in her eyes and in the tiny quiver of her lips. But alongside that, Rahim read fear, stark and real.

A lesser man would have been thrilled to be in the position to leverage her actions against her both publicly and privately. To pay her back for daring to invade his thoughts day and night where no other woman had consumed him with such fervour. But all Rahim wanted was to be alone with her. To test this insane attraction and see if it was as real as his mind and body insisted it was.

He would satisfy himself that Allegra Di Sione was forgettable. Then he would show her the progress he'd made in the past two months in Dar-Aman. It was strictly a matter of pride that she not continue to believe that he was content to live in his opulent palace while his people suffered from his father's neglect.

The moment her speech was over, he surged from his seat. He waited, hands clenched by his sides as the room erupted in rapturous applause. Again her gaze cut to him, wary questions chasing through the blue depths, before quickly skittering away.

He followed her slender figure as she returned to her seat. Impatiently, he waited as the chairman officially closed the conference before he mounted the podium to where Allegra was indulging in photo ops with a few first ladies. Uncaring about the flashing camera, he cut through the throng surrounding her and stopped in front of her.

Her sleek head turned towards him, and Rahim knew, in that moment, he hadn't exaggerated the powerful chemistry between them. Every fibre in his body hungered for her with a desperation that was blindingly visceral.

'Allegra,' he rasped her name, and just the act of doing so seemed to expand the pressure in his chest.

'Y-Your Highness. I wasn't informed you would be attending this conference, or I would have made time to meet with you...'

The formal address, falling so stiffly from her lips, made him want to pull her close, take her mouth in a ruthless kiss and shame her for daring to keep him at arm's length.

'Make time now.' Rahim made sure his tone conveyed he wasn't making a polite request. 'I insist.'

She glanced beyond his shoulder and spotted the two

burly bodyguards behind him. Her vivid apprehension thickened, reached out and curled around them.

'I can't just…leave,' she parried.

Rahim raised a mocking brow. 'I think we both know you can do *exactly* that.'

Every last trace of colour fled her face. Her lashes swept down and she breathed deep before she looked up at him. Against his will, he devoured her lovely features, cursing himself for being *this* captivated with her despite all she'd done.

His breath caught as she took a step closer and leaned towards him. 'I can't do this here, Rahim. Please,' she whispered shakily.

He caught the delicate scent of her perfume, felt the heat radiating off her body and reined in enough control not to reach out and pull her tight against him. 'Then leave with me. We're going to talk, Allegra. It's your choice whether you want an audience or not. You're an intelligent woman. Choose the latter.'

She swallowed, and stepped back. Glancing to the side, she smiled at a younger woman who hurried forward. 'Zara, please cancel my lunch appointment, and send my apologies to Lady Sarafina.'

Her assistant tried to hide her surprise, and failed. 'I… Yes, of course. Should I cancel the press junkets too?'

Allegra glanced at him, a thousand questions in her eyes. Rahim stared back, biting down the uncivilised growl that threatened to erupt from him. He'd never been possessive about any of the women who'd passed through his life. And yet, the thought of sharing Allegra with anyone sent a pulse of deep displeasure through him. Adding caveman to the list of unpleasant characteristics he'd had to acknowledge since meeting Allegra Di Sione made his teeth clench.

She caught the look, and quickly nodded at Zara. 'Yes, reschedule those for tomorrow.'

Rahim barely saw the assistant melting away. He saw nothing and no one except Allegra. When she turned to leave the conference room, he followed.

Her stylish navy dress and matching jacket clung to her body as she walked beside him. Rahim watched her smile in acknowledgement at several people, her movements displaying a regal grace that would make his king-makers proud.

From nowhere, he wondered what his mother would've thought of her. Would the queen who'd lived most of her life as a fairy tale have taken to Allegra? Or would she have feared for her son and the near-obsessive emotions bubbling through him right now?

Slashing through the fog of futile musings, he crossed the grand foyer of the five-star hotel and inserted the key-card for his private lift.

'Um…where are we going?' Allegra asked.

He tried his best to ignore the wariness in her voice. 'To my penthouse. It's the only place we'll be guaranteed complete privacy.'

'There are offices reserved down here for the conference. I'm sure we can find one that isn't occupied.'

He faced her as the lift doors opened. 'Why, Allegra, are you suddenly afraid to be alone with me? Do you fear for your reputation, perhaps?' he mocked.

The firm shake of her head belied the racing pulse at her throat. 'No, I merely thought it would be expedient. You seem in a hurry.'

'Oh, I am in a great hurry. I cannot wait a moment longer to find out how you thought you'd get away with stealing from me when you knew there was nowhere you could hide that I wouldn't find you.'

She inhaled sharply and glanced over her shoulder. Only his bodyguards were within eavesdropping distance. With a wave of his hand, Rahim dismissed them. And then did what he'd been dying to do since he walked into the conference room two hours ago. He reached out and grasped Allegra's wrist. She resisted for a tiny second before joining him in the lift.

Passing the keycard over the LED monitor, he watched her swallow as the doors sealed them in. Silence surged along with the lift. Sliding his hand up her arm and over her shoulder, he caught a finger under her chin. 'Look at me, Allegra.'

Stunning blue eyes met his.

'I asked you a question. Answer me.'

Her mouth worked for a moment before she answered. 'I tried to pay you for what I took. I sent you five cheques. They were all returned, ripped in pieces.'

Rahim allowed himself a tiny, mirthless smile. 'Not only did you grossly insult me by stealing from me, you then presumed to know the value of my possession?'

She shook her head. 'I didn't just pluck a number out of thin air. I...I had the box appraised. Discreetly, of course,' she added, then flushed when he laughed.

'Of course. How very thoughtful of you.'

A pained expression crossed her face, then the apprehension he was beginning to detest gripped her features once more. 'I know there's no excuse for what I did...'

'None whatsoever,' he agreed. Drawing his finger over her smooth jaw, he revelled for a stolen second in the silky warmth of her skin.

'I made a promise to my grandfather, Rahim. One I couldn't break.'

He stiffened. 'And did the great Giovanni Di Sione condone the theft?'

She gasped. 'Of course he didn't! He never would.'

'So you not only perpetrated a crime against me, you risked bringing dishonour to your family in the process?'

Pain twisted her features. 'I'm sorry it happened,

Rahim. Truly, I am. But when, right from the start, my visit went badly, I had very little choice but to…'

'Seduce me with the enchanting delights of your sexy body, then steal away like a thief in the night?' The harsh reminder roughened his voice.

Impossibly, she went even paler, and it was then Rahim pulled back and took a closer look at her.

'What have you been doing to yourself? You've lost weight.' He took in her deathly pale complexion, her slightly hollower cheeks and the bruised shadows beneath her eyes. 'Have you been ill?' he demanded sharply.

The lift doors slid open directly into the Emperor Suite. She stumbled out and away from him, shaking her head as she put the width of the living room between them. 'Not exactly, no.'

A cold spear lanced his spine, far too close to what he'd felt a long time ago, when his pregnant mother had been rushed to hospital, for it to sit well with him. 'What sort of answer is that? Either you've been well or unwell. There's no in between. What happened?'

She threw out her hands in a stalling gesture. 'Please. Slow down.' One hand went to her forehead and Rahim reeled in shock when he noticed that her whole body was trembling. He found the idea that he'd caused that reaction deeply unsettling.

Crossing over to where she stood, he caught her by the shoulders. 'Tell me what's wrong, Allegra. Now.'

The eyes she raised to his were almost navy with fear and worry, clouded with whatever inner demons chased her, and he watched, his shock escalating by the second, as she blinked back sudden tears. 'I can't…I can't go to prison,' she stammered.

He frowned. 'I don't recall threatening you with incarceration,' he replied.

Her hands braced on his chest, her gaze imploring. 'I

stole from you. It can't be a coincidence that the moment I stopped sending the cheques, you appeared. You want some sort of retribution for what I did…'

'Perhaps. Perhaps not.' Rahim refused to admit to a certain compulsion in checking his mail once Allegra had started sending the offensive cheques. With each one, she'd written a small note expressing her remorse for what she'd done. He'd been mildly disconcerted when they'd stopped coming, as if a tenuous tie had been severed.

'Why are you here, Rahim?' she asked, her voice stronger now. As if she'd talked herself into facing him and whatever consequences her actions would bring.

'I'm here because your actions need answering.' *And because I can't stop craving you.*

His arms dropped like leaden weights as the unspoken words seeped like poison inside him. He'd jumped on his private jet and travelled thousands of miles at a time when his people should come first. And although the reason for his being here was for his people, he couldn't deny that seeing Allegra in the flesh came a very close second.

The similarity between his actions and how his own father had allowed Dar-Aman to fall to ruin because he'd been consumed by his mother powered through Rahim. He took a step back from her, then several. Finally he whirled and paced to the window.

No, he *wasn't* like his father. Khalid Al-Hadi had allowed so-called love to weaken him to the point where he'd been unable to function once he'd lost the object of that love to complications in childbirth. Neither his kingdom nor his *living* first-born son had been worth rallying himself from the pathetic depths of despair for.

Rahim had watched his loving father turn into a husk so swiftly and completely that he might as well have been buried alongside his wife and unborn child.

It had taken long, hell-raising years before Rahim had

accepted that his father had had no room in his heart for the son that lived. The only abiding emotion had been the grief that consumed him.

No, he was nothing like his father. He had never wanted a woman badly enough to contemplate throwing away everything for her. He never would.

'Rahim?'

He swerved from the view, his fingers spiking through his hair as he fought the tentacles of memory.

'I came here to set a few things straight with you,' he sneered, deeply resentful that she'd led him to question himself when there was no doubt where his destiny lay. 'You thought what happened in Dar-Aman wouldn't go unchallenged. You were wrong.'

Allegra's hand jerked to her stomach, her eyes more vivid against her ashen colour. 'No. Please…'

From across the room, Rahim saw her sway. With a curse, he charged forward and caught her as her legs gave way. It occurred to him then that she hadn't answered him when he'd asked what ailed her. Swinging her up in his arms, he carried her to the sofa and laid her down.

With a low moan, she tried to get up. Rahim stayed her with a firm hand. 'I'm going to get you some water. Then you'll tell me what's wrong with you. And what the hell you're doing giving long speeches and photo ops when you should be in bed.'

Her mouth pursed mutinously for a moment before she gave a small nod.

Rising, he crossed to the bar and poured a glass of water. She'd sat up by the time he returned. Silently she took the water and sipped, her wary eyes following him as he sat on the sturdy coffee table directly in front of her.

'Now, tell me what's wrong with you.'

The sleek knot at her nape had come undone during the journey to the sofa, and twin falls of chocolate brown hair framed her face as she bent her head. Rahim gritted his teeth against the urge to brush it back, soothe whatever was troubling her, reassure her that he meant her no harm.

He was so busy fighting his baser urges, and sternly reminding himself that he was in the right, and *she* in the wrong, that he didn't hear her whispered words.

'What did you say?'

Her jerky inhale wobbled the glass in her hands. 'I said I'm not sick, but I can't go to prison because I'm pregnant.' She raised her head then, and stared back at him with eyes black with despair. 'I'm carrying your child, Rahim.'

CHAPTER TEN

WITH THE LIFE-ALTERING words uttered, Allegra held her breath, expecting the world to crash around her. After all, who would want a virtual stranger with questionable integrity to suddenly announce they were to be the mother of your unborn child in a little over seven months?

Allegra hadn't quite got over her shock of seeing Rahim again. She'd barely been able to keep it together on the stage after spotting him seated right in front of her, his body draped in a three-piece designer suit, and his face draped in volcanic rage.

Conducting her speech, knowing she faced an epic battle for survival that could very well end her once the conference was over, had been the most difficult thing Allegra had done.

Or so she'd thought...

At the continued thick silence that chilled her to the soul, Allegra glanced up. 'Say something. Please.'

Rahim's face was frozen. And ashen. Only his eyes moved. They searched her face, then dropped to her stomach for several tense heartbeats, before they snapped back up.

'You're pregnant.' His voice was a rough husk, all emotion bled from it. 'With my child. My heir?'

'Y-yes.'

He jumped to his feet, paced with jerky strides to the opposite sofa. Shrugging off his bespoke Savile Row suit jacket, he flung it down. His vest and pinstripe tie met the same fate. Then he was heading back for her, his face an icy, furious mask as he bent towards her, hands planted on either side of her. 'We created a child together two months ago…and you were planning on telling me *when*?' Eyes like twin black vortices filled her with blinding dread.

Allegra nervously licked her lips. 'I'd planned to get in touch after the conference.'

'Because your schedule was too tight in the *eight weeks* prior to make time to deliver the news to the father of your child?' he blazed down at her.

'I didn't find out until last month,' she retorted.

He gave a single dismissive shake of his head. 'Don't hide behind semantics. Did you plan this?' he grated.

She sucked in a horrified breath. 'No!'

'So we find ourselves in the position of being the one percent of individuals to suffer a failure of contraception.' His eyes darkened and he straightened to his full, regal and bristling height. 'Nevertheless, Allegra, you've known for a *whole month*.'

'And it's been a month of hell, I assure you,' she countered before she could stop herself. 'Don't think I've had it easy, Rahim.'

He stilled, his gaze narrow-eyed and piercing. 'Define *hell*, if you please.'

Despite the insanity of her situation, her pulse tripped at the exotic intonation of Rahim's words. 'You mean besides the twenty-four-hour nausea and the knowing I'd have to account to you at some point for what I did? Or that my child would suffer for any mistakes I make?'

'Explain,' he reiterated. 'Make me understand how anything less than a personal catastrophe that rendered you deaf, dumb and blind excuses you from not telling me the moment you found out.'

'How about being terrified that I'll be a terrible parent?'

she slashed back, her innate flaw that had lived with her for so long surging to the surface.

He propped his hands on his lean hips, a frown still wedged firmly between his brows. 'I may be wrong in my assumption, but I doubt that expectant parents get the perfect blueprint detailing their potential brilliance in child rearing.'

'Perhaps not, but templates matter. Whether we like it or not our pasts have a direct bearing on our future. It was why I never wanted children.'

Colour leached from his usually vibrant complexion. 'You want to get rid of the baby?' he whispered jaggedly.

'No!' Allegra's hand shot up, the very thought of *not* having this baby growing inside her filling her with desperate desolation. 'It was what I believed I wanted before this happened. But now it's here…I want it more than anything. Please believe me.'

Rahim swallowed hard, his chest moving deeply as he exhaled. 'I'm sure you'll agree that asking me to believe you on anything will be a leap for me. How do I know you won't change your mind again a week or two down the road?' he asked imperiously from his eagle-eyed stance across the room.

'I won't!' Her hand cradled her flat belly, her words and gesture both woefully inadequate against the ire raining down on her.

'And I'm just to take your word for it? After you've admitted contemplating not having children in the first place?'

Allegra scrambled round for the words to explain how she felt without exposing herself and her many flaws. 'That was because I don't know… I don't think I'll be a good mother, Rahim. Some women are built to be mothers. I'm not one of them.'

'Why not? Because you take drugs on a regular basis,

perhaps?' he asked. 'Tear around New York City while off your head with booze, hurling abuse at every child you come across?'

'Of course not!'

'Do you plan to?' he pressed.

'Don't be ridiculous, Rahim.' She stopped and calmed herself down. 'I had planned to tell you about the baby, but I wasn't sure how you would take it...whether you'd even *want* this child, especially...'

'Especially what?'

Her breath stuttered in her lungs. 'With me as its mother.'

He regarded her for a solid minute. His square jaw tilted upward, his whole body vibrating with suppressed anger. 'I am a *sheikh*, Allegra, and you're carrying the heir to my throne. That is the situation we find ourselves in. Wishing the reality we're faced with to be different is a futile exercise.'

Like a moth seeking a deadly flame, Allegra wanted to ask him to state in plain terms what he truly believed— that given the choice his heir would've been born by a different woman. A suitable woman. But she pulled back at the last moment, the sick dread and pain dredging through her already too much.

'There is only one way to take this. For me to be fully involved in our child's life,' he stressed.

'Rahim...'

'There's nothing more to say on the subject. If you truly want this child, then the only way is forward.' Rahim's frowning glance raked her from head to foot. 'Is the morning sickness the reason you've lost so much weight?'

She shrugged. 'I guess.'

'And you didn't think to cancel this conference?'

'I'm pregnant, Rahim, not suffering from a debilitating illness. This conference was important. Maybe even to Dar-Aman...'

His head snapped up as if she'd offended him. 'I see we're back to dangling empty promises.'

She sat forward and set the glass on the table. 'It's not an empty promise. I've done some more research since I got back. I think I can help the situation in Dar-Aman.' She thought about what he was asking, and took a risky gamble. 'If you could see it in your heart to let my grand-father keep the box, I'll give you whatever...'

'I don't give a damn about the infernal box! Dammit, Allegra, you're carrying my child. You think I care about a blasted trinket?'

'I don't know. Do you?' she countered, unable to come right out and ask how he felt about the baby, besides the imperious and proprietorial claim he'd made on it.

A single Arabic curse vaulted from his lips and he re-sumed pacing.

Allegra stared, heart in her mouth, as he caught the top button of his pristine white shirt and ripped it open. His chest heaved, as if he was gripped in a fever. For endless minutes, he paced a tight circle in front of her. Just when she thought he'd rip a hole in the carpet, he snatched up his jacket.

'I need to get out of here.'

The breath exploded from her lungs at the thought that he was leaving. 'What?'

He launched a tight-lipped smile. 'Don't worry, I'll be back. And just in case you get it into your head to sneak off, I'll be posting a bodyguard outside your suite. For your sake, I hope you don't attempt anything foolhardy.'

Allegra opened her mouth, but no words emerged. The sheer volley of emotions wrung from her in the past hour seemed to have affected her ability to speak. Silently, she watched him stab his arms through his jacket sleeves, the raised collar bracing his nape. For the first time since she met Rahim Al-Hadi, he looked dishevelled, but God, even that state was dangerously sexy enough to trigger a series of ripples through her belly.

Her breathing altered, her pulse racing wildly as her gaze raked upward from his washboard torso, past his broad shoulders to his mouth.

When her gaze clashed with his, Rahim froze, his eyes darkening dramatically as the air thickened and pulsed with volatile sensual charges.

Pushing back the heavy fall of her hair, Allegra licked her tingling lower lip, the need cloying through her body almost unbearable.

'Rahim...'

'Careful,' he growled. 'You're in no state to issue invitations with your eyes that your body can't handle, *habibi*. And I'm in no state to be gentle with you. Stay put. Rest. If you need anything, Ahmed will be right outside. Or pick up the phone and dial my personal butler. But you are not to leave this suite. Is that understood?'

Annoyance at his high-handedness snapped her spine straight, the lust wearing off a little. 'You can't keep me prisoner here, Rahim.'

He raised sleek eyebrows. 'Are you absolutely certain about that?'

She gasped, but he was striding to the door. Before she could blink, he was gone. She sank back against the plush sofa, deflated and exhausted, her mind whirling at a thousand miles an hour.

The only way is forward...

Allegra had no idea what those words meant. But what she did know was that nothing about her pregnancy had brought Rahim anything even close to joy. His shocking disbelief, followed by a rigid acceptance, had done nothing to allay her own fears of the role her heart was already embracing but logic insisted she would fail at.

Despair crushed harder, brimming her eyes with hopeless tears. She brushed them away, but they surged again.

She knew how transient life could be. How volatile and uncertain.

She was bringing a child into this world without knowing its father's true feelings about being a parent, or even what he intended to do with the bombshell she'd dropped at his feet. Besides staking his ownership of their child, Rahim had done very little else.

And there was still the issue over the stolen Fabergé box. Allegra groaned and stretched out on the sofa. She was trapped here till Rahim returned. She could either wallow in despair, or use the time to make further plans for her child's future. Now that Rahim knew about the baby, there was the equally daunting matter of telling her family.

She would tell them…as soon as she found a way to prevent Rahim from sending her to jail for stealing!

Rahim cradled the single-malt Scotch in his hand, his gaze lost in the swirls of the amber liquid. He had yet to take a drink in the six hours since he entered the private gentlemen's club in the exclusive street in Geneva.

He was to become a father.

His level of alarm wasn't as catastrophic as he'd imagined it would be. But neither had he believed a single night of madness would set his life on this roller-coaster path.

And he'd yet to formulate a different plan than the single one blazing a path through his brain.

In all things he made contingencies but for this he had none. Allegra was pregnant with his child. A child whose blood was already stamped with the same destiny Rahim had been born with. A child whose gestation and eventual birth carried the same risks his mother had been subjected to.

The hand clutching his crystal tumbler shook. He tightened his grip and threw back the drink, welcoming its bracing sting.

Glancing up for the first time in hours, Rahim saw that the club had filled. He recognised a few faces but didn't return the greetings nodded his way. The scowl on his face discouraged patronage, but it drove home the fact that he was recognised wherever he went in the world. People had seen him with Allegra, both in Dar-Aman and here in Geneva. Rahim had made it his business to confirm she hadn't dated anyone in the past two months. Once evidence of her pregnancy became public knowledge, it wouldn't take a genius to work out he was the father of her child. Not that he intended to hide that fact.

Which brought him to the matter of how his subjects would take a child born out of wedlock. His people had been through the wringer economically and even socially.

What kind of ruler would he be to throw another scandal into their lives when they were reeling from the legacy his father had left them with? Not to mention the further damage to his personal reputation that could set back months of negotiation for a better future for his people.

He shook his head as his personal valet stepped forward bearing the silver tray that held the Scotch bottle. Rahim shook his head, knowing his choices couldn't be found in drink. But the more he stared into the bottom of the empty glass, the larger the answer blazed.

For his heir.

For his people.

For himself.

There was only one choice.

'Marry me.'

The shock wave that powered through her made Allegra grip the cushion beneath her as she struggled upright. The magazine she'd fallen asleep leafing through fell to the floor. 'Rahim, you're back!'

'Marry me.'

'What?'

Rahim stood before her, still in his jacket, his hair spiked in all directions, like he'd run his fingers through it many times. 'You're carrying my child.'

'So?' she squeaked, her mind scrambling past the visual wallop he packed just by being him.

Eyes turned a burnished bronze blazed at her. 'Marry me.'

Numbly she shook her head, the few words she'd managed so far the extent of her vocal ability as she tried to absorb what Rahim had just asked of her. She was still shaking her head when he reached forward and cupped her jaw.

'If you have arguments, speak them now.'

Hysteria bubbled up inside her. Frantically, she tried to pull herself together, speak the words that would restore sanity. 'I can't.'

His grip tightened. Imperceptibly. But she felt it. And she saw the cold withdrawal in his eyes before he freed her.

Turning, he strode to the bar set on the far side of the elegant living room, and poured a shot of amber liquor. Throwing it back, he rolled the side of the glass over his lips before he set it down with a sharp click.

Slowly he strolled back to her. Despite the steady, unhurried pace, Allegra's spine tingled with dread.

'Are you prepared to lose everything you've spent your life building without due consideration?' he enquired casually, his balled fists sliding into his pockets.

'What are you talking about?'

'I'm talking about your foundation. Your freedom.'

Ice-cold fear climbed into her throat. 'My *freedom*?'

'Once the disappearance of the box is discovered, you can be assured charges will be brought.'

Allegra gasped. 'You said you didn't give a damn about the box,' she muttered through frozen lips.

A hard light momentarily gleamed in his eyes. 'I don't. But there are others who do. It wasn't just a personal possession you stole. Before my mother died, she expressed a wish to have her collection made a national treasure, to be displayed in the Dar-Aman National Museum upon her death. My father could never bring himself to honour that wish.' His face tightened for a moment before his features neutralised. 'As Dar-Aman's ruler, the collection is now mine. I've had my hands full with other matters of state to get it done. But my mother's wish is one I intend to honour in the coming months. The theft of such a treasure is an offence punishable by a lengthy prison term.'

Panic clawed through her. 'And how does marrying you change my fate?'

He shrugged. 'As my queen you'd have to answer to no one. The box can be my wedding gift to you. Marry me, and your grandfather need not lose his precious keepsake. Your foundation will continue to thrive, free from the scandal that could see all your hard work turned to dust overnight. My people won't have to suffer the consequence of the scandal of an illegitimate child. And most importantly, our child won't suffer the stain of being called illegitimate. He or she will be my true heir, with an unchallenged birthright.'

The calculated way he enumerated his wishes chilled her soul. On the one hand, she knew he was offering her personal salvation and a safe start to her child's life. And yet, looking at him, seeing no softness in Rahim, her heart dropped to her stomach.

Was this to be another failure to add to her ever growing list? In the hours since Rahim had left her alone, she'd tried to convince herself she could do this alone, if need be. After all, millions of women had succeeded, hadn't they? But now Allegra realised that she hadn't really believed herself. What she'd hoped for was a sign that Rahim would be willing to undertake this journey with her, not out of duty but because a part of him, no matter how small, wanted this child too. Looking at him now, fresh doubts flooded her.

Her parents had provided legitimacy and the occasional bout of twisted affection and nothing much else. Allegra knew the fierce glow that burned within her each time she thought of the child growing in her womb was a different emotion to what she'd experienced as a child. It was even different from what she felt for her siblings.

It was deeper, and fiercely intense. One that she would lay down her life to protect.

But would it thrive in an atmosphere filled with recrimination? Like her parents, would that love eventually become distorted once she accepted a ring from a man she barely knew? A man whose sole reason for being here was duty?

'Allegra.'

She looked at Rahim. 'Was this why you left? To make this cold and calculating plan?'

His face hardened further, drawing a shiver from her. 'Our marriage won't be cold and calculating. Only the planning and execution of it.'

'Is that supposed to reassure me?'

'You're a pragmatist, Allegra. Same as I. We are faced with a situation and we have to find the best way forward. This is the *only* way forward.'

No mention of love. No mention of hearts and roses. Allegra told herself it wasn't what she'd expected anyway. She didn't fool herself for a moment into thinking Rahim would feel the same newly discovered love she felt for the baby growing inside her.

But even as the alien hurt lodged itself in her chest, she forced herself to think past it. She reminded herself that to Rahim she was a stranger. Yet he was willing to tie himself to a woman he'd had a one-night stand with for a lifetime. Even if it was just for the sake of their child, it was a huge sacrifice. One she couldn't dismiss out of hand.

And as calculating as it seemed, perhaps she was better off halving the risk of failing as a mother with Rahim by her side rather than not. He had known a better childhood than her…could perhaps even find affection for his child once it was born…

The endless darting thoughts ground to a halt when his hands jerked out of his pockets and he stormed forward. 'Allegra…you *do* want this baby, don't you? You haven't changed your mind?' The question fired from him, white-hot and bullet sharp.

Seeing the lethal tension spiking higher by the second, Allegra swallowed. Surely if he felt this strongly and was still concerned about what her decisions were about this child they hadn't planned, then it was a good start?

'I haven't changed my mind, Rahim. I want this baby.' The belief that she could make this work settled deep inside her.

He exhaled, the tension slowly draining out of him. Then he nodded. 'Good,' he gritted out.

Although she accepted rationally that she couldn't hold it against him, a tiny part of her soul still withered at the matter-of-fact way he'd set the course for the rest of their lives.

Allegra had pushed any thoughts of settling down far out of her mind when she realised she wouldn't be mother or wife material a long time ago. But there'd been times as a child when she'd dream of her fairy-tale prince.

Rahim Al-Hadi was as regal and princely as they came. But she knew this was as far from her childhood fairy tale as she could get. She'd taken all the wrong turns to get to this destination.

And while she was being offered a chance to make the best of a bad situation, what exactly did being the wife of a sheikh entail?

'I won't stop my work with the Di Sione Foundation.' That was non-negotiable, notwithstanding her actions having placed her career and any future good she'd hoped to do in a precarious position. Her foundation work had been her saviour when every other aspect of her existence had been a grey wasteland. She had her child to think of now, but her work was equally as important.

He nodded. 'Of course. I've appointed a few more women ministers in the past month. I hope you'll work with them to see to it that Dar-Amanian women achieve the same rights as their male counterparts?'

Allegra felt her eyes widen. 'You've done that already?'

He shrugged. 'The process had already begun when you visited my kingdom. Had you not had your own agenda, perhaps you would've found out for yourself.'

Shame drenched her. Before she could find words to appease him, he continued. 'I need a yes, Allegra.' His gaze caught and locked on hers, a ruthless compulsion in the hazel depths. 'A yes that you'll *mean* come tomorrow morning.'

The reminder that she'd fled in the night after promising to stay made her flush. She wanted to look away, but that would show weakness. And she couldn't be weak. Not when it came to such an important decision.

Taking a deep breath, she passed a soothing hand over a stomach swarming with butterflies. 'Yes, Rahim. I'll marry you.'

He stared at her for several seconds, then he took an

equally deep breath before exhaling. 'There must be no delay. There'll be enough questions as it is when you deliver in seven months.'

'Really, people still question legitimacy based on a nine-month conception within marriage?' she asked cynically.

Rahim summoned a ghost of a smile. 'In many ways I'm as western as you are, but unfortunately, I can't speak for all of my kingdom. Best we don't set too many tongues wagging. Dar-Aman can't afford another scandal right now.'

Allegra was reminded then the many times Rahim had spoken of his people when she'd been in Dar-Aman. She'd been too clouded with her own judgements to hear the affection and devotion in his voice when he spoke of his subjects. But now she knew better.

And everything *she* did from here on would also reflect on his people.

Swallowing the nerves, she rose from the chair. His keen eyes watched warily. 'I'm fine,' she said hastily when he took a step towards her. She didn't want him close. So far she'd been able to retain enough rationality to make the vital decisions. Allegra didn't think she'd be able to progress as effectively if he stood close enough to touch, to smell. She had a hard enough time not devouring him with her eyes.

She'd thought he looked beyond exceptional in a traditional *abaya*. Seeing him in clothes that accentuated his honed body so sensationally was a weakness on her system she couldn't allow. Not when that look of hungry lust they'd shared before he left in the middle of the afternoon still tugged relentlessly at her.

'So what happens now?' she asked, desperately wresting back the practical side of her nature that seemed to have deserted her.

'I inform my council of my intention, and they will take it from there. I expect the date will be within the week.'

'A *week*?' She didn't realise she'd swayed again, until he caught her arms. His touch was as electrifying as it'd been this afternoon. But this time self-preservation made her resist.

He tightened his grip. 'Dammit! Stop fighting me. And don't tell me you're only pregnant, not sick. Ahmed tells me you didn't eat anything on the tray the butler brought you. You're so weak you can barely stand on your own two feet. I'm calling a doctor.' Taking a step forward, he placed her back on the sofa.

'Rahim...'

He silenced her with a hard kiss, gone almost before it'd arrived, but no less stimulating. 'No. You're a modern woman who can work hard and play harder with the best of them. I get it. But you're carrying my child, Allegra. And if you think I'm going to stay quiet or stand down when it's obvious you're unwell, you can think again. You'll receive the best care from a team of doctors while you're carrying this baby. That is *completely* non-negotiable.' There was a raw and unshakeable resolve in his voice that dried any protests she may have had. But it was the almost too carefully disguised note of fear in his voice that caught and held her attention.

It urged her not to stand in his way. After all, the baby's health and safety was just as important to her. 'Okay,' she conceded.

Nodding, he reached for his phone. After a five-minute conversation conducted in rapid-fire French, he ended the call. 'The doctors are on their way.'

She also found out just how invested Rahim was in his child when a team of four doctors and two medical technicians walked into the suite an hour later. Allegra's eyes widened when the sonogram was wheeled in.

Once she'd been quizzed thoroughly on her medical history, Rahim dismissed all but one doctor and technician, then took her hand and led her to the master bedroom.

A medical robe had been left on the bed, and he picked it up, a look of anxiety crossing his face again. 'I leave for Dar-Aman tonight. Before I do, I'd like to hear my child's heartbeat. If you don't mind?' The guttural request lanced her heart, sparking warmth that radiated outward until it engulfed her whole body. For one blinding second, Allegra hoped for the impossible—that this child had been conceived via the fairy-tale love she'd once dreamed about. Recognising the wish for the foolish act it was, she pushed it away, and embraced the real gift being handed her.

'I'd really love that, Rahim.'

His smile was blinding, heart-stopping. Nodding, he handed her the robe, left the suite and returned a few minutes later with the doctor and technician.

Allegra had thought Rahim would remain standing, but he got into bed with her, and slid in close. His warmth and scent engulfed her, pushing that wish once again to the fore. When he caught and held her hand as the gel was spread on her stomach, she carefully avoided looking into his face. She was too afraid her own would give too much away. So she held her breath and trained her gaze on the monitor as the probe glided over her belly.

After several minutes of silence, a strong heartbeat filled the room, followed a moment later by a grainy picture on the monitor. Allegra gasped, pure joy racing through her bloodstream.

Rahim made a rough sound, and her head swung to him, the vow not to look at him so much dust in the face of the transcendental moment they were caught in.

'Is everything all right?' he jerked out, the hand holding hers almost punishing in his grip.

The doctor nodded. 'Yes, it's a little too early to tell the sex, but everything is as it should be, Your Highness.'

Exhaling a breath she hadn't realised she held, Allegra glanced back at Rahim. A fierce light burned in his eyes as he looked from her face back to the machine. As he stared at the image, a transformation seemed to come over him. The apprehension she'd glimpsed on and off since announcing her pregnancy flashed over his face one last time. Then his features settled into stony determination. Allegra felt his withdrawal seconds before he dropped her hand, slid off the bed and accepted his copy of the ultrasound picture.

'Rahim?'

He didn't answer, just continued to stare at the picture as slowly, inexorably, a new and even more terrifying tension enveloped him.

'Rahim, are you okay?' She raised her voice, alarm catching hold of her.

His gaze jerked to hers, and his mouth compressed. 'All will be well. *Insh'allah*,' he said, his voice deep and powerfully final. Sliding the Polaroid into his pocket, he walked out of the room.

The vow was still echoing in her head when she'd dressed and left the bedroom ten minutes later. Something urged her to seek an explanation for Rahim's unsettling reaction. For the fleeting glimpses of fear she'd seen on his face.

Entering the living room, she opened her mouth to ask, then turned in surprise as loud voices, punctuated with several belligerent hammers, sounded on the door.

Rahim exchanged puzzled glances with her before issuing an order in Arabic. A bodyguard entered, followed immediately by a severely irritated Bianca.

Before she could get a word in, her sister emerged from behind the burly minder and spotted her.

'Oh, thank God, Allegra. I've been searching for you everywhere! Zara said you cancelled your afternoon appointments and left with some guy. That was almost eight hours ago. I was worried when you didn't answer your phone.'

Before Allegra could reassure her, Rahim spoke. 'Your sister has been otherwise engaged. And as you can see for yourself, she's completely unharmed.'

The firm authority in Rahim's tone made Bianca blink. She studied him properly for the first time, her eyes widening as she took in the powerful man before her. 'Who are you, and why are you holding my sister here?' she demanded, although her voice was less confrontational.

'I am Sheikh Rahim Al-Hadi of Dar-Aman. Your future brother-in-law,' he replied, his voice a steely vibration that coated the words in unmistakeable power.

Bianca's folded arms dropped, along with her jaw. Swallowing, she shook her head. 'No way,' she whispered.

His lips compressed. 'Perhaps you'd care to seek verification from your sister, and offer her your support once you have done so.'

Bianca turned, wide-eyed, to her. Allegra nodded. 'It's true. Rahim and I are getting married.'

For several seconds, silence reigned. Allegra could almost see the questions tearing across Bianca's mind like the adverts that lit up Times Square. But her sister hadn't attained stellar success as a PR guru without mastering the art of discretion.

With one final look between Rahim and her, Bianca, still dazed, murmured, 'Then you have my support. And I guess I'm also going shopping for a new dress?'

CHAPTER ELEVEN

RAHIM HAD VERY little recollection of leaving the hotel room and boarding his plane back to Dar-Aman. But he could very much recall Allegra's face when he'd told her he was leaving. The questions in her eyes which he'd glimpsed on her emergence from the master suite had given way to relief.

He'd known she was curious about his reaction to the picture burning a hole in his pocket. But how could he offer explanation without sounding like a paranoid freak?

How could he tell her that once again he feared his life had been set on a course that could alter his very future? What man would want to tell the woman who carried his child that he was terrified beyond understanding of anything going wrong? Of lightning striking twice and plunging his world once more into darkness?

Besides, what would telling Allegra about his emotions surrounding his mother's death or the brother he'd lost before he was even born achieve?

What he needed to do was to ensure the preparations for the wedding got under way without delay. Before the relief he'd seen on Allegra's face coalesced into foundations for doubt about marrying him. Settling back in his seat as his pilot readied for take-off, Rahim wished that he was anonymous and could whisk her off to Vegas for a shotgun wedding performed by an Elvis impersonator.

He smiled grimly. He wished for many things, but each one was tossed aside for the futile nonsense it was.

He wasn't an ordinary man, and nothing but a Dar-Aman marriage ceremony, undertaken according to his ancestors' coronation laws and duly consummated, would ensure his child's legitimacy. He hadn't planned on becoming a father this soon. Truth be told, he'd pushed that particular fulfilment of his duty to the bottom of his list when, with each liaison, he'd doubted his ability to find a woman worthy of being his queen. No woman had been worthy of being what the Dar-Aman people deserved.

But Allegra would be.

He'd seen how much the Nur-Aman people had taken to her. And her belligerent anger over the neglect his kingdom had suffered pointed to a care and concern that wasn't a disguise.

On top of that, she wasn't distracted by fairy-tale stories of profound love and loss the way some women were. Allegra Di Sione was practical, her breeding and intelligence grounding forces which would be nothing but a huge benefit for Dar-Aman. For him.

Slowly, he pulled the ultrasound scan from his pocket. He examined each pixel of the frame, then started over again, passing his thumb several times over the smooth surface.

As for the fierce pounding of his heart, he thought as his thumb caressed the glossy image one last time, it was adequate concern for the well-being of his child. A natural reaction to the frailty Allegra had exhibited.

What had happened to his mother wouldn't happen to Allegra. Or their child.

All will be well. Insh'allah.

'You brought Alessandro with you?'

Bianca grimaced and carefully avoided Allegra's eyes

in the mirror. Her other siblings had called over the past six days in answer to the news of her impending marriage. Each call had expressed their woefully disguised surprise at her uncharacteristic decision. Alessandro had been particularly sceptical, but Allegra had dealt with her lone-wolf brother for long enough to know the right words to say to him to curb any suspicions he might have.

She'd thought she'd succeeded. Alessandro's presence here indicated otherwise.

Bianca shrugged and adjusted the heavy gold necklace adorning Allegra's neck a careful fraction. 'He just gave me a ride on his jet. He was…in the area.'

'Bianca…'

'What? Ally, come on, give me a break. You've always been the practical, head-screwed-on-straight one out of all of us. And yet you've known this guy for, what, five minutes? And you're marrying him? Something's obviously up, but I know better than to judge.'

Something was definitely up. For one thing, Rahim had been avoiding her since she reached Dar-Aman. She didn't understand why, nor could she deal with the almost physical pain not seeing him brought her. 'So you brought Alessandro to do it for you?' she demanded.

Her sister shrugged again. 'He's just giving him a quick once-over.'

Allegra disguised the shaking in her hand by unnecessarily tweaking her headdress. 'Rahim's the sheikh of Dar-Aman, not a racehorse.'

Bianca tutted. 'He's also scary, in a drop-dead hot sort of way. I needed backup in case you were being strong-armed into doing this. How well do you know him anyway?'

It was Allegra's turn to avoid her sister's gaze. 'I'm not being strong-armed.' Not much anyway. She feared her unknown future as a wife, a queen and a mother. But the first step—marrying Rahim—was now an inevitability she couldn't alter. The ceremony itself was daunting enough without borrowing future trouble.

Like answering how well she knew her future husband.

Her heart lurched as she silently answered—*not very well*. She'd barely spoken to or seen him between his abrupt departure on the evening of her conference and her subsequent arrival in Dar-Aman two days ago. The Marriage and Coronation Council, as they'd called themselves, had flown to New York when Allegra had told them there was no way she could drop everything and return to Dar-Aman on one day's notice. They'd invaded her office, throwing a normally calm and efficient Zara into bewildered chaos, until Allegra had had no choice but to send her assistant home.

With Di Sione Foundation matters temporarily passed to her second-in-command, Allegra had been whisked back to Dar-Aman and thrown into a protocol initiation that had made her head spin.

But even mentally exhausted, Allegra had been able to see the further changes which had occurred since her visit two months ago. More building works had sprung up in Shar-el-Aman. The squares were less crowded with disgruntled citizens who now had jobs to fulfil them. And when the motorcade carrying Allegra to and from her whirlwind appointments with women's organisations went past, both young and old cheered, despite not knowing who rode within the blacked-out confines of the limo.

The further extensive changes Rahim had made in the short time since she'd mistakenly condemned him were truly impressive.

But there was one matter she wasn't pleased about. One thing that needed addressing before she married the ruler of Dar-Aman. And with her sister lingering she couldn't make the call.

'This is my decision, Bianca. I'm at peace with it. That's all you need to know, okay?' The gravity of her reply had the effect she wanted.

Bianca exhaled and nodded. 'I'll see you at the ceremony, then.'

Allegra kept the smile on her face until Bianca shut the door behind her. Then she lifted her gaze to the mirror once more.

She barely recognised herself beneath the heavy make-up and the royal gold-and-blue headdress pinned into place by the dozen women who'd dressed her an hour ago. Her blue eyes shone wide and exotic, rimmed with delicate kohl and gold eyeshadow. Her mouth was painted with a special lip balm said to have been harvested from a sacred tree that bloomed once a year in the Dar-Aman desert. Carefully licking her lower lip, Allegra tasted the exotic spice of the balm. The same precious leaves had been crushed into a pulp and used to henna her hands and feet.

In fact, from head to toe, she'd been transformed into a bejewelled creature she didn't recognise. No wonder Bianca was concerned.

But while Allegra was uncertain about what the future held, she knew one thing she absolutely couldn't tolerate. Lifting the phone on the dresser, she dialled.

'The office of Sheikh Al-Hadi. How many I help you?' came a voice quite different from her future husband's.

The depth of her disappointment was keen and sharp. 'Hi...' She floundered. 'This is Allegra... Di Sione. Can I speak to Rahim?' she asked of Rahim's personal aide.

'Excuse me one moment, please.'

Her hand tightened on the phone as voices murmured in the background. A full minute passed before the personal aide self-consciously cleared his throat. 'I'm very sorry, Miss Di Sione, but His Highness is indisposed at present. He expresses his apologies.'

Pain lanced her, along with jagged anger. 'Are you sure he expresses his apologies, or are you expressing it on his behalf?' she shot back, very much aware she was shooting the messenger, but unable to stem the dread and bewilderment tightening into a hard knot in her chest.

'I… Yes…of course…'

'Oh, never mind.' She hung up before she could make a further fool of herself.

She wished she could get up and walk out of the palatial suite that was every princess's dream come true. Out of this fairy-tale palace. Out of Dar-Aman. But Allegra knew she wouldn't. For the sake of her baby, she had to do this.

She had to marry a man who kept a harem right under her very nose!

A sob caught in her throat, but she swallowed it quickly as a soft knock sounded on the door and jerked her further into a reality filled with trepidation.

'Mistress, the procession is ready for you,' Nura announced, her smile stretched wide as she hurried to Allegra.

'Thank you, Nura,' she struggled to reply.

Allegra rose from the centuries-old 'betrothal stool' she'd been placed on and waited quietly as Nura arranged the heavy fall of the blue silk behind her, before slipping her feet into flat, ruby-encrusted golden slippers. The royal-blue gown threaded with gold matched her headdress. With wide sleeves and a fitted bodice, it flared in a stiff skirt to stop a few inches above the floor, so the jewels adorning her ankles and feet could be seen when she moved.

The double doors to her suite opened when she neared, and half a dozen women who'd been with her since sunrise curtsied deep, then began chanting the pre-wedding incantations.

Allegra had wondered why the women who'd dressed

her had insisted on giving her the customary hour on her own before the ceremony began. Now she knew. Only her mind wasn't at ease at all. The mental nail-biting and butterflies-battling had increased a hundredfold.

She hadn't been able to help her mother or her siblings when they'd needed her. But with the different perspective provided ironically by Rahim, she could begin to forgive herself for her failure in that regard. As for helping the women in Dar-Aman, she was also confident her help would be welcome, even valuable.

And as Rahim had pointed out, as queen, she would be even more influential in helping to bring about change. Perhaps she'd been wrong to condemn herself so soon. Perhaps she'd needed Rahim to show her that *this* was her time to make a true difference.

It was the role of wife she feared most. She had no idea how she could be Rahim's wife when she didn't know what he expected of her. And she certainly wasn't about to share his bed when he planned to share himself with others!

In less than an hour, she would no longer be Allegra Di Sione, but Her Royal Highness, Allegra Al-Hadi, Queen of Dar-Aman.

And she was already failing at that! Because she knew she would never be the kind of wife who would blithely look the other way while her husband lay with other women.

She wanted to be the *only* woman he took to his bed. His only wife. And she wanted Rahim as her husband. Her true husband. The admission shook her to the core, even as the cruel reminder that Rahim's sole reason for marrying her had been to secure legitimacy for his heir and to please his people struck deep.

Anguish slashing through her, Allegra's steps faltered as they reached the edge of the western wing. Through a large Moorish archway, a gold carpeted walkway led to the palace's private beach. Rose and jasmine petals had been strewn along the way. The part of her that wasn't reeling with deep apprehension took in the sheer beauty of the ceremony and logged it away in her memory banks.

Beyond the boundaries of the no-fly zone Nura had excitedly pointed out to her, news helicopters from around the globe hovered.

She was concentrating on putting one foot in front of the other when a tall shadow detached from the VIP guests lining the walkway to follow her down to the beach. Her breath caught as Alessandro stopped in front of her.

'Allegra.' His voice was firm, but his eyes bore into hers with brusque concern which warmed her.

'Alex. Bianca told me you were here.'

He frowned. 'Are you sure about this?'

Beneath the folds of her gown, she crossed her fingers and pushed down the overwhelming panic and despair. 'Yes, I'm sure,' she said in as firm a voice as she could muster.

Her brother stared at her for another brooding minute, then nodded. 'Then you have my blessing. And Grandfather's too.'

Allegra glanced at Bianca, who'd joined them, then back at Alessandro. 'You weren't just in the area, were you?'

He shook his head. 'No. The old man sent me.'

Despite her clogged throat, Allegra summoned a smile. 'Thank you.'

With another nod, her brother stepped back into his place in the crowd.

The end of the walkway loomed and the chanting stopped. Yasmina, the head of her wedding entourage, turned and gestured to her feet.

Wordlessly, Allegra took off the golden slippers. Yasmina picked them up and stepped to the side.

'You make the journey alone from here.'

Heart in her throat, Allegra glanced down the endless flight of steps.

On the beach, wearing a blue and gold *abaya* and matching *keffiyeh* held in place by silk rope, stood Rahim. His eyes were trained on her, his frame tall and proud, his demeanour set in stone.

A shift registered deep in her soul, pressing home that there was no turning back. Whether she wanted it or not, Rahim was her destiny.

On bare feet, she glided down the stairs and paused at the edge of the carpet.

At the instruction of the three elders officiating the ceremony, Rahim strode forward. Stopping in front of her, he removed his own jewelled slippers and stepped barefoot on the carpet next to her.

Wordlessly, he held out his hand and she placed hers within it. Warm and strong, his hand gripped hers, setting off fresh nerves, and a horde of new butterflies.

She glanced up at him, and darkened hazel eyes bore implacably into hers.

'We do this part together.'

Shakily she nodded and stepped off the carpet onto the warm, coarse sand with Rahim.

The elder moved forward and uttered words she didn't understand. Opening an ancient book, he extracted a long, braided rope and nodded at Rahim. He spoke his vows in Dar-Amanian, his voice firm and deep. Then Allegra repeated the words she'd learned in the language of the kingdom she was about to dedicate her life to.

Rahim held her steady and the rope was bound around their clasped hands from her wrist to his.

'Now in English, so there is no misunderstanding,' Rahim commanded.

Allegra swallowed. 'In the presence of the sand, sea and sky, I pledge myself to you. My honour, my body, my soul.'

Rahim's gaze pinned hers. 'In the presence of the sand, sea and sky, I pledge myself to you. My honour, my body, my kingdom.'

And with those handful of words, they were married.

'Where are we going?' Allegra asked, although she half suspected the answer.

Behind the wheel of the sturdy Jeep, Rahim navigated another shadowy sand dune, one of many they'd encountered since their journey from the palace straight after the wedding feast.

'Dar-Amanian wedding custom dictates that a bride spend a secluded night in a Bedouin tent with her groom,' he replied, his eyes on the road before them.

He'd barely spoken to her, except to introduce her to their most distinguished guests during the wedding reception. All through the ceremony, he'd conversed with his ministers, then their guests. But to her, he remained polite and courteous, but distant. And she hadn't had much to contribute in the way of conversation, consumed as she was by what the future held. And the very vivid, unacceptable subject of his harem.

Her stomach roiled as she struggled to answer. 'Yes, I know that from the giant book I had to study in twenty-four hours. Same way I know that the royal bride has a two-week grace period before her coronation for the night to happen.' She certainly wasn't in a hurry to grace Rahim's bed, not when the thought of him choosing another bed in the near future stabbed like a hot knife between her ribs.

'That grace period was to accommodate monthly issues that no longer apply to you since you're already carrying my child. I did not see the need to wait,' he stated.

Allegra's head snapped round to him as she caught the thick pulse of lust in his voice. She was fiercely glad the interior of the Jeep was dark and he couldn't see her un-guarded reaction to that lust. Or the need for it to be solely *hers*. 'I didn't think…we didn't discuss anything about the physical part of our marriage.'

'What is there to discuss?' he demanded.

She gave a shocked laugh. 'A lot, I should imagine. Or did you think I would accept the status quo without question?'

He directed a frown at her. 'What are you talking about?'

'Why did you not take my call this afternoon, before the wedding?' she slammed back, the hurt she'd tried her best to gloss over gaping wider.

'I was busy,' he replied.

'Too busy to make time for your fiancée?' She shut her eyes for a second, as if it would block out the need she could hear in her own voice.

A tense silence greeted her, his face a stark profile. 'I assumed it was pre-wedding jitters prompting the call. Since we are now married, I'm inclined to think we're past those reasons.'

'You assumed wrong. We're most certainly *not*.' Her hands tightened in her lap, a new and sharper pain lancing her when she considered what she'd do if he refused what she was about to request. Sadly, her response, should he refuse, would be definitive.

'I'm listening, *habibi*.'

She sucked in a steadying breath. 'I need you to close the east wing.'

'What?' The puzzlement in his voice squeezed at her heart.

'Shut down your harem, or we won't be consummat-ing this wedding.'

'*My*…? Where did you get the idea that I had a harem?' he bit out.

'Please, Rahim…don't toy with me. This isn't something I intend to live with. I don't care if you threaten me with jail. Promiscuity isn't part of this marriage deal.'

'Allegra, be quiet for a second,' he inserted harshly after navigating another steep dune and bringing the Jeep to a stop.

Silence broken only by the exotic sound of desert creatures drenched them. Her hands squeezed tighter, her whole body vibrating as she waited for him to continue.

'I don't know where you got the idea from, but there is no harem. Not in the east wing, not in the whole palace. My father was a one-woman man and so was my grandfather. I intend to be the same. The only woman who will be servicing me in bed is you. The east wing is used to house female undergraduates who form part of the internship programme to complement their hospitality degrees at Dar-Aman University. The male students are housed in another wing in the palace.'

She gaped at him, the sheer relief pounding through her rendering her speechless for several heartbeats. 'I… What?'

He repeated what he'd said, his voice deep and powerful. Eyes the colour of a Dar-Amanian sunset gleamed at her. 'You're welcome to interview the students yourself if you don't believe me.'

Slightly dazed, she shook her head. 'That…won't be necessary.'

'So you don't wish me to shut it down?' he mocked.

Heat flared up her face. 'No. Of course not. But can you blame me for asking?' she murmured.

'No, but the lingering of certain preconceived notions could become a problem for us. Now was there anything else you wished to threaten me with on our wedding day?' he finished, his voice holding a lethal calm she'd only witnessed once—in his study on her last night in Dar-Aman two months ago when she'd accused him of neglecting his kingdom.

Biting her lip, Allegra knew she had to make things right, but for the life of her, she couldn't think how. 'Rahim…'

He started the Jeep and the powerful vehicle rolled forward. 'You have uttered the vows and taken my name, *habibi*. This is now beyond you and me. Now you know your imagined harem doesn't exist, you have no excuse. We *will* consummate this marriage. You belong to me, and I fully intend to claim you again.'

Allegra didn't see the need to argue the possessive point because she *wanted* to be claimed. She wanted to belong. Now that the subject of other women had been nullified, the thought of belonging to Rahim didn't terrify her as much as it would've only a short while ago.

It was what made her reply, 'You can claim me all you want. As long as I get to claim you too.'

In the darkness, his eyes gleamed. His response was an animalistic growl as he stepped on the gas, steering the Jeep with a deft confidence that she wasn't ashamed to admit turned her on despite the roiling sensations tearing through her.

The lone Bedouin tent appeared out of thin air.

Two stories high, the tent was large enough to fit the huge Di Sione pool back on Long Island. The canvas was made of traditional Dar-Amanian blues and gold, and had been opened up to reveal its warm, lantern-lit interior.

Rahim parked the Jeep in front of it, and came round to help her out.

Sliding her body down his, he speared his fingers into her hair and gazed deep into her eyes. 'You're mine now. There will be no room for suspicion and uncertainty. The past needs to belong in the past.'

She knew he referred to her issue with the harem. 'But

because this marriage isn't a dictatorship, I hope my concerns will be addressed appropriately?'

'They will be, if you bring them to me immediately and not let them fester for weeks,' he muttered.

'I tried. You wouldn't take my call.'

'You had every chance to speak to me long before this afternoon, did you not?' he rebuked.

'Fine. I'm sorry about that. Can I make it up to you?' she offered boldly as she swayed against him, his proximity, and the need clawing through her, too overwhelming to deny.

'Yes, *habibi*. You may,' he instructed thickly.

He barely allowed her the kiss she tried to initiate before he sealed his mouth, hot and fast, to hers. His tongue delved between her lips to boldly capture hers, the expert, demanding flicks telling her how much he wanted her.

When he finally lifted his head, she was near-drowsy with desire.

'I've been dying to do that since you walked down the beach to me,' he muttered.

Her arms tightened around his neck, just to keep upright. 'Why didn't you, then?'

'I wouldn't have been able to stop once I started. And I didn't think you'd welcome me scandalising you in front of your brother and sister.'

Leaning up, she pressed her lips against his in gratitude. 'Thank you. Did Alessandro give you a hard time?'

Rahim's mouth twitched. 'We made sure we understood each other. But enough about that. We're here now, and I can't wait to have you naked and beneath me.'

His pure male growl as he swung her into his arms thrilled her blood. His kiss as he carried her into their oasis paradise threatened to send her into orbit. Setting her down next to a low, wide bed covered with a dozen cushions, he undressed her in sure but hurried movements. Then stood back and watched her.

'They say a pregnant woman has a special glow about her. But you, my enchanting bride, transcend beauty itself,' he said, his voice almost worshipful as his gaze raked her from head to toe and back again.

Allegra swayed to him, her hands sliding over his broad shoulders as he groaned, laid her down on the bed and wrapped her naked form in his arms. Allegra was sure the boom of fireworks in the distance was her senses detonating at the sexual skill her husband wielded over her. Everywhere he touched, her body heated, then melted under his attention. Almost in direct opposition, his body tensed with each touch, his erection growing harder and thicker with each slide of her leg against him.

Suddenly, he reared back from her. Stalking to the myriad lamps dotted around the vast space, he turned them all off except the one on their bedside table. He started disrobing as he made his way back to her. By the time he reached the bedside, her husband was gloriously naked and utterly captivating.

Shamelessly, she arched her body and reached up for him. 'Rahim, I want you.'

'And I *need* you. Now, please, *ya galbi*, before I explode!'

Sliding between her thighs, he kissed his way down her throat to her sensitive breasts. Despite the tension whipping through him, he took his time, moulding and caressing her, until she begged him to stop torturing her. But he merely transferred his attention lower, stopping to plant reverent kisses on her belly before he parted her thighs with a firm demand.

Rahim showed her just how potent a lover he was. By the time he reared up over her, Allegra was near-delirious with ecstasy. But she knew she wasn't complete.

Not until he truly made her his.

Finally, he surged inside her. His name spilled from her lips in a stifled scream. He exhaled harshly, his mouth searing across hers before he thrust home again.

'Allegra, my beauty,' he groaned against her ear as he sent them both higher.

'Rahim…'

'Your husband,' he croaked, the command clear.

'My husband,' she obeyed, laying herself wide open to the spiritual sealing of their commitment.

Then she was soaring, her heart already halfway to delivering itself to the man who owned her. That she wanted nothing more than to place it at his feet right then should've been the first sign that she was falling in love with Rahim.

But Allegra was too wrapped up in bliss to care. After they fell back to earth, she opened her eyes to a renewed brightness in the tent.

'I thought you turned the lights down?' Her voice was a husky slur.

Rahim reached out and turned the glare back down. 'I had to turn it back up for a moment?'

She stared back at him. '*Had* to?'

He smiled. 'A short evidence of the marriage's consummation.'

Allegra felt her face flame as she recalled that part of the traditional ceremony. 'Oh, God! Our silhouettes against the tent?'

He nodded, laughing at her horror.

'How many people will be watching?'

He shrugged. 'No one will confirm it but at least one or two of the elders will be on the mountain to witness our joining. Maybe more.'

As if on cue, another boom sounded, this time much closer to the tent. 'What does that mean?'

'Our union has been approved.'

Minutes later, Rahim was still chuckling at her embarrassment. Rising, he filled a platter with the food that had been laid on a low table in the sitting area. After feeding her dates, sun-ripened tomatoes and stuffed vine leaves, he disposed of the dishes, came back to bed and pulled her into his arms.

Settling deeper into the bliss that flowed from her soul, Allegra combed her fingers through his hair, more content than she'd ever been in her life.

'Your beautiful eyes have lost focus. What's on your mind, *habibi*?' he enquired after a few minutes of peaceful silence.

'I've never believed in fate and destiny. But after everything that's happened to us…' Her voice drifted off, her fear that she would reveal too much and drive him away a living thing inside her.

'And you believe it now?'

'My grandfather believed in hard work and ambition… or so I thought until recently.'

Rahim leaned back and stared down at her. 'What are you saying?'

She cupped his jaw, revelling in the rough maleness of his skin. 'Today, it occurred to me that everything I've done has led me here. It may sound absurd, but I can't help but think I'm right where I need to be.'

Leaning down, he kissed her long and deep. Then he caught her closer to him, his strong arms wrapping her tight…tighter, until their hearts echoed one another's, then beat as one.

'It's not absurd, *ya galbi*. Not absurd at all.'

At dawn, Allegra rose to use the bathroom. Smiling at Rahim's disgruntled protest to her leaving the bed, she entered the luxurious bathroom and crossed to the stall. She wasn't certain what made her look down.

The blood on her thighs didn't make sense at first. She

was carrying the child of her heart. *Fate* itself had handed her this precious gift.

But then she remembered that until today she'd never truly believed in fate. Fate had only ever *taken* from her, not given. It'd taken her parents. It was stealing her grandfather right from under her helpless nose.

And now it was about to take her very soul.

'*Rahim!*'

CHAPTER TWELVE

RAHIM JERKED AWAKE, his blood curdling as it always did each time he dreamed of her screaming his name. Sweat dripping from his brow, he rose from his narrow cot and stumbled to the window. The view over the racetrack was the same as it had been yesterday and the day before that. Last week, it'd been views over the cratered land mass that constituted the rejuvenated oil fields in the northernmost point of Dar-Aman. In the three weeks before it'd been over different sites just like these.

The work involved with rebuilding his kingdom was unrelenting and punishing. And he welcomed every second of it. He needed the punishment. Because with each tunnel dug or brick laid with his bare hands, Rahim could reward himself with taking another breath, knowing he was atoning in some small way for his hubris.

How many times had he condemned his father for the same mistakes he'd ended up making?

He'd arrogantly believed he could have it all. Allegra. His child. His kingdom.

His wedding night had showed him just how wrong he could be.

Rahim had believed he'd found a way to taste happiness without losing his heart or his head. When Allegra had spoken of fate and paths taken, he'd even begun to let go of the anger he'd felt for his father, while patting himself on the back for getting it right this time. He'd taken every precaution he could. Allegra's doctors had assured him his new wife and the baby were both fine. That he could enjoy his wedding night like any newlywed. Heaven had beckoned and he'd lost his mind.

Just like his father had believed he could have it all, once upon a time, Rahim had started dreaming of forever, forgetting that in one single night Khalid Al-Hadi had lost everything. Including the son whose face he hadn't been able to stomach looking at because he reminded him of his loss.

Rahim knew all this, and yet he'd put himself at the same risk, and placed Allegra and their baby's well-being on the line through his greedy yearning for what he shouldn't have craved in the first place.

Laying his head against the cool glass of the nearly completed paddock VIP suite's window, he tried to stem the other conversations running through his head.

Striding to the phone next to his sleeping place, he punched the numbers.

The voice that answered was groggy and disgruntled.

'I need an update on how the latest ultrasound went.'

Frantic scrambling in the background proceeded a halting, '*Your Highness?* A thousand pardons but it is the middle of the night.' At Rahim's terse silence, more scrambling ensued. 'Please hold on, Your Highness... I'll just grab the notes.'

Irrational rage flared up his spine. 'You mean you can't remember results of a test you conducted just this afternoon?'

'Please, Your Highness, I have it.' The doctor cleared his throat. 'Both child and mother are in excellent health. The pregnancy is thriving.'

Rahim allowed the veiled implication that others were *not* thriving sail over his head. 'And?'

'I'm sorry, Your...?'

'How did my wife look?' Rahim cut across him. 'Did she look happy? Worried?' Was she as breathtaking as she'd looked that last time they'd made love? Right before he'd allowed thoughts of hearts and fairy tales to break down his carefully erected barriers? Noting the thickening silence, his hand tightened around the phone. 'Did you not understand my question?'

'I...I'm sorry to report that Her Highness believed she felt the baby kick for the first time while I was performing the ultrasound.'

'What do you mean she *believed*? Are you calling my wife a liar?' Rahim grated.

'No! Never, Your Highness. But in most cases, it's too early to feel any kicking yet. But she was quite adamant.'

A vice tightened around Rahim's chest and his vision blurred. 'Was she pleased?' he whispered.

'I thought she was, but then she burst into tears. She was quite inconsolable.'

'When is her next check-up?'

'In two weeks, Your High...'

Rahim hung up and dropped to the ground, his skin scraping along the raw concrete floor. The phone clattered away, but he barely heard it.

The thought of the strong, capable woman he'd married reduced to crying alone in her private clinic tore at him in ways Rahim would've given anything not to feel.

But he felt each tear like a knife slashing across his skin, the pain engulfing him, drowning him. Panic flared through him, wild and unfettered. Ruthlessly he reminded himself that this was why he'd left Shar-el-Aman. So he could endure the pain.

He *would* withstand the pain. And he would stay away from Allegra and the baby.

He had to. The alternative was unthinkable.

* * *

'What's next on the agenda?' Allegra looked around the conference room, trying to keep her smile pinned in place. But these days when breathing felt like an extracurricular activity, smiling featured even lower on the unending to-do list that came with being queen.

'The Hamdi sisters have petitioned for help again,' Yasmina informed the group.

'Have we had any success locating their errant husbands?'

'No, our investigators believe they've fled the country with their company's embezzled funds. Oh, and His Highness wants to sit in on any further meetings regarding the Hamdi sisters.'

Allegra tensed at the mention of her husband's name. 'Why?' she snapped.

Yasmina looked up warily. 'He went to university with the younger sister's husband. I think he feels responsible...'

Allegra couldn't stop the bitter laugh from escaping. 'He feels responsible for a situation he had no hand in creating?'

Yasmina shrugged. 'I'm sorry, those are his instructions.'

'Well, he's not here to enforce them, is he?' Her snap cracked a little this time, and her throat tightened in warning of tears.

Two of the women seated at the table exchanged wary glances.

'Is that all?' Allegra asked.

At the affirmative answer, she rose, pinned a smile on her face again and walked out with the ten businesswomen comprising the newly formed Dar-Aman Women's Foundation.

The moment she reached the hallway leading to the royal wing, she fled, desperate to get away before the floodgates opened. Lately, they'd taken to bursting wide open when she least expected it. Like this morning, when she'd spotted a bird with feathers the same colour as Rahim's eyes. She'd cried for an hour straight in the royal suite she'd slept in alone for the past three and a half weeks.

All because she'd lost her heart on her wedding night to a husband who had no use for it.

At first Allegra had thought Rahim had been worried about the baby. Even after the doctor had reassured them that her condition was nothing more than a little spotting since her wedding night had fallen on the same day her period normally came, Rahim had been adamant that she be admitted to hospital and monitored for another forty-eight hours. She'd lain there in blissful ignorance of the fact that her husband was laying tracks to absent himself from her life.

Her phone call to him once she'd returned and he'd still kept away after a week, to ask when he was coming home, had been the most humiliating ten minutes of her life. The only saving grace had been biting her tongue before she made the folly of telling him she needed him home because she'd fallen in love with him. That was a secret she intended to take to her grave. Or channel into the already overflowing love for her baby.

Allegra stopped in the doorway to her bedroom, and gasped as the fluttering the doctor had blatantly disbelieved she was experiencing beat its tiny wings in her belly.

The wonder of it never got old. Kicking off her navy shoes and matching jacket, she got into bed and lay on her back, her hands cradling her small bump. As if waiting for just that act, the fluttering came again.

'Oh.' And just like that, tears filled her eyes. She allowed herself a short cry this time, then rolled over and picked up the bedside phone.

Punching in the number she knew by heart despite having used it only twice, she gripped the handset and waited.

'Hello?' Rahim's voice was harshly gruff, dripping with impatience.

'Rahim…it's me… Allegra.'

'You think I wouldn't recognise the voice of my queen?'

'I don't know. I don't seem to know much these days.'

'What do you want, Allegra?'

She laughed, the sound scraping her throat. 'Are you sure you want an answer to that?'

His tense silence spoke volumes.

'I guess I should get to the point. Will you be attending the fundraiser for the schools in the northern district tomorrow night as you promised last month, or am I expected to attend another event alone and make your excuses, *again*?'

'Harun will let you know.'

Her throat threatened to close up. 'You know what? Don't bother. I'll go on the premise that I'll be attending alone. If you turn up, it'll be a happy surprise for your adoring subjects, I'm sure.'

She slammed the phone down a second before the tears came. Clutching the pillow, she cried until her temples ached and her heart bled. After dragging herself to the shower, she slid into bed, thankful when she grew drowsy immediately. But of course, like clockwork, she dreamed of Rahim, and their night in the Bedouin tent, before the fleeting happiness she'd known had been snatched.

And when she woke with tears in her eyes, she determinedly brushed them away and prepared for the day ahead.

Making sure to take lengthy breaks and conducting her meetings from the office set up in the palace, she returned to her suite at five, conferring with her stylist over what to wear to the fundraiser before heading for the shower.

An hour later, dressed in a blood-red silk gown with criss-crossing shoulder straps, with a clutch and shoes to match, she slid into the back of the royal limo.

Her first hint that she wasn't alone was the heart-wrenchingly familiar scent that hit her nostrils before she turned to find her husband lounging in the far corner.

'Rahim!' She couldn't help but drink him in, her senses jumping to high alert as they absorbed the long-denied visual of her husband. His hair had grown at the back, almost covering his nape. His cheeks were shrunken and his body was a sleeker version of the man she'd married. But he was still impossibly handsome, so breathtakingly masculine, he aroused every cell in her body. 'What… You came…'

'As you said, I made a promise. Put your seat belt on, Allegra.'

She complied, fighting to breathe around the hot arrows shredding her heart. 'And what makes this particular promise worth keeping and others not?'

In the semidarkness, his jaw clenched tight. 'Perhaps this was a mistake.'

'No! The mistake is you thinking that what you're doing isn't hurting this marriage. Or the people you claim to care about so much. Or do you think the work is done simply because you put a ring on my finger and a baby in my belly?' Her voice rose, every miserable day she'd spent without him seeking redress.

'Allegra, calm down…'

'Don't tell me to calm down! You asked me to bring my concerns to you. Well, *you're* my concern. Your absence from our home, from our marriage bed, from our baby's life, is my concern.'

His head went back, the streetlamps dotted along the highway throwing his features into intermittent light and dark. 'I can't be in your life, or the baby's, while you're pregnant. I can't be around you. The risk to you both is too much.'

'But that's not all, is it? Please don't insult my intelligence by denying that there isn't more going on. You've shut me out completely, and you won't tell me why. Did I do something?' she pressed, willing to ditch her pride for a minute if that's what it took.

Rahim shut his eyes in a pained grimace. 'I can't do this now, Allegra. But no, you didn't do anything.'

'And that's all I'm going to get? The *it's not you, it's me* line?'

'We're here, so unless you want to take this outside, I suggest we shelve it.'

The Rolls glided to a perfect halt on the edge of the red carpet of the five-star hotel where the fundraiser was taking place. As patron and guest of honour, she and Rahim's much desired presence was being televised.

Knowing she had less than ten seconds before the driver opened her door, she turned to her husband, and gave in to the urge to touch him. Placing her hand on his arm, he stalled his forward movement. 'There are only so many things you can stick up on a shelf before the whole thing comes crashing down, Rahim. I want to make this work, but it won't as long as you keep shutting me down.'

The door opened before she could insist on a reply. With no choice but to force a smile and face the six-deep paparazzi, Allegra slid into her role.

She was still smiling three hours later when the auction part of the evening ended, raising three times more than the charity had hoped for. When the string quartet struck up a waltz, she granted a dance to the prime minister of Dar-Aman's neighbouring state.

Halfway through the song, she stiffened slightly as Rahim strode through the dance floor and stopped beside them.

'I hope you don't mind, but I need my wife back.'

'Of course,' the older man replied, smiling fondly at them before heading back to the table.

'How well you seem to fool everyone,' she muttered, willing herself not to lean into the body she'd missed more than she knew was healthy for her.

She felt a sigh move through him, then the whisper of air against her neck as he drew her closer. Despite her best efforts, both her heart and body leapt with foolish joy.

'I know you think I'm staying away to make you suffer. But I'm not. I only have your best interest and that of our child at heart. You just have to trust me.'

'It's hard to do when you won't talk to me, Rahim. Something happened in Geneva when you saw the first sonogram.'

'I wasn't expecting to be a father. Chalk it up to being overwhelmed.'

The song ended and she drew back more than a little forcefully from him, exasperation and anguish eating her alive. 'Lie to yourself if you want, but don't lie to me.' She kept her voice low so she wouldn't be overheard. 'When you're ready to let me in, I'll be at our home. The one you insist on running away from.'

She turned and walked from the dance floor. The moment the end-of-evening speech was done, she gathered her clutch and wrap and headed for the door.

Rahim helped her into the car and slid in beside her. Neither of them spoke as they drove away from the hotel. She was so busy fighting the tears that she started when she noticed they'd pulled up at the royal private airport.

On the tarmac, Rahim's private chopper slowly powered up. She told herself she wouldn't look at him, or acknowledge his departure.

But she couldn't help herself, especially when his gaze focused on her, compelled her to look at him. His eyes burned with almost demonic intensity, and when his gaze dropped to her mouth, it was all she could do not cry out and beg him to stay.

'Take care of yourself and our baby, *ya galbi*. I'll be in touch soon.'

Alighting with lithe grace, he turned to slam the door. She blocked it with a firm hand. 'If you expect me to smile and say, "Yes, husband, go with my blessing," you're in for a nasty surprise. You don't have my blessing to go, Rahim. All you're doing is making me hate you more for what you're doing to us. Is that what you want?'

A touch of his vibrant colour receded. His lips firmed but she was past caring. 'I don't need your permission to carry out my duty. Go home, Allegra. We will resolve this when I return.' He turned and started to walk away.

She refused to con herself into not caring any more. The truth was that she cared. Far too much to stand this ravaging pain any longer.

Rahim didn't love her.

Most times during the past weeks those four words had cut her in half. Other times she'd assured herself she was better off with a man who would disappear for weeks rather than face her and tell her he didn't return her feelings. That her talk of fate and being where she was meant to be would never include him in any way but as the father of her baby.

Either of those states of being hadn't stopped her from missing him *all* the time.

Which was why the thought of him walking away from her one more time shredded her heart. It was why she leapt out of the car and slammed the door shut.

He whirled around, his eyes widening. 'What are you doing?' he shouted over the loud *thwopping* of the chopper blades.

'If you won't stay and talk to me, then I'm coming with you,' she yelled back.

He lunged forward the same time she quickened her steps. With the manufactured wind whipping at her evening gown, Allegra couldn't gather it out of the way in time to keep her heel from catching in the hem.

She stumbled forward.

She managed to brace her fall with one hand, her palm scraping painfully along the tarmac before he snatched her up. 'For God's sake, are you *insane*?'

'Yes. I'm off-my-head crazy, and it's all your fault!' she blurted before her voice fractured.

He swung her into his arms, his strides swift and urgent as he carried her back to the car.

'Yes, I'm aware everything bad that has happened to us is my fault, but that is no reason to put yourself and the baby in danger.' His voice was a thin, desolate line that cut her to the heart.

She glanced up at him, and noticed he'd lost every trace of colour. His eyes when he looked down at her as he deposited her in the seat were bleak, black pools.

Heart wrenching at his obvious distress, she murmured, 'I'm fine, Rahim.'

He slid in beside her and secured her seat belt. Without answering he pressed the intercom and issued terse instructions. As the limo rolled away from the chopper, he picked up her hand and gazed at the blood seeping from her cuts. 'I beg to differ, Allegra,' he drawled. Taking a handkerchief from his jacket, he pressed it against the small wounds. 'Consider your point well made.'

She gasped. 'You think I did this deliberately?'

He shrugged. 'You wanted my attention. Now you have it.'

Allegra wanted to scream with despair. She wanted to close her eyes and absorb that deep, sexily exotic voice and fool herself into believing everything would be all right. Most of all, she wanted to weep with joy that Rahim was here with her, touching her, albeit under harrowing circumstances.

But, *dammit*, she'd wept far too much lately. And all the reasons revolved around him. She snatched her hand from his, ignoring the throbbing in her palm.

'Think what you like. It's obvious I'm fighting a losing battle.' Desperate for him not to witness how much those words hurt she glanced out of the window, saw where the limo had stopped on the palace grounds. 'Why are we at the clinic?'

'You just suffered a fall. You don't think it prudent to check that you and the baby are fine?' His tone held the same bleakness that lingered in his eyes, laced with a vulnerability Allegra had never heard before.

Her heart cracked but she reminded herself that Rahim was doing this for the baby. Before she could answer, the door opened. Her doctors and nurses swarmed the car.

She was ushered inside the private clinic Rahim had had created for her. A nurse saw to her hand as the doctors consulted in hushed tones. Through it all, Rahim stayed aloof, his expression unreadable as she was prepared for her scan.

The realisation that she hadn't got through to him shook hard through her. She knew in her bones that the moment the scan was over, he would leave. And she would once again become the broken, pathetic creature who craved him to live.

No.

No more.

She didn't care what it took. She was taking back her power.

Strolling to the curtain where she would be changing into her gown shortly, she glanced casually over her shoulder. 'So where will you be heading to this time once this is over? Vietnam or the wilds of Scotland?'

His eyes stayed on the monitor, his folded arms tensing as he shifted on his feet. Somewhere along the line, his bow tie had come free, along with his two top buttons. Allegra forced her gaze away from the strong column of his throat and concentrated on removing the evening gown.

'The Port of Dar-Aman. Berthing contracts were sold to foreign entities. I'm in the process of buying them all back.'

'And you need to do that three hundred miles from home?'

'Yes.' Simple. Succinct. Cutting.

She got the message. But she was getting angrier by the minute. With herself. With him, for her inability to stem the waves of pain that hurled relentlessly at her.

Taking deep, calming breaths, Allegra met his gaze over the screen, and asked the question she'd been holding to her breast like a precious talisman which might crumble to dust any minute.

'Why didn't you tell me your mother died in childbirth?'

Rahim jerked from the wall, his eyes full of warning as he glared at her. 'Because it wasn't a subject I felt should be shared with a pregnant woman.'

'What about your *wife*?'

His lips pursed. 'You seem to be spoiling for a fight, *habibi.*'

'Since when is wanting to know a few basic facts about the man you're married to spoiling for a fight?'

He sighed and dragged his hands down his face. 'You know enough about my parents. Why is this further questioning necessary?'

'Because we agreed to discuss things before we jump to conclusions, remember? Of course you'd have to actually be here for any discussion to happen.'

Tension tightened his body. 'You have a palace and every luxury at your disposal. Surely you can't feel that neglected?'

Anger and pain rearing up like two coiled snakes, she stalked to where he stood. 'How about you stop second-guessing my feelings and have a frank discussion with me? Or is this something else you want to *shelve*?'

'I won't have a discussion with you about what happened to my mother. What would that achieve?'

Something inside her broke right then. 'I can't believe you'd ask me that,' she whispered raggedly.

A flash of something close to pain tightened his features. Then he looked away.

She was staring at him, wondering what to say, when her team of doctors returned. The nurse sent to help her took over when Allegra's hands shook too badly to don the clinic gown. On wooden legs, she returned to the ultrasound room and lay on the bed while the gel was spread over her stomach. Over her shoulder, Rahim's tense presence bore down on her.

'Since Her Highness was due to come in tomorrow anyway, we'll make sure everything's fine first, then take some measurements, Your Highness. It shouldn't be too long.'

The process took less than ten minutes, but it felt like forever. 'Everything's fine with the baby, and with you too, Your Highness.' The doctor smiled at her.

Allegra heard Rahim's shaky exhalation and she swallowed the painful lump in her throat, unable to suppress the wish that his relief was for her too, and not just their baby.

Averting her gaze from him, she blinked back threatening tears as another doctor stepped forward. 'I don't believe you've seen a 3D image of the royal baby yet. Since you're both here, we thought it would be the perfect time?'

Her breath caught, but before she could agree, Rahim rasped, 'Will it hurt the baby or my wife?'

'No, Your Highness. It's not harmful.'

Rahim must have nodded, because the equipment was

swiftly set up and Allegra positioned in place. She felt rather than saw Rahim step closer.

At the first picture of their son, he inhaled sharply. A second later, his hand gripped her shoulder. Her heart flipping up from where it'd fallen to her stomach, she reached up. He meshed his fingers with hers and they watched as the image was rotated to show their healthy, thriving baby.

'He's beautiful,' Rahim murmured.

'Yes,' she agreed.

She looked up and his gaze connected with her, the emotion in his eyes naked and raw. They stared at each other until a throat cleared—the medical team was stepping outside.

Rahim's withdrawal was swift and complete, like a sheet of bracing cold water thrown over her. The roar of pain filled her ears as she swung her legs over the side of the bed and watched Rahim heading for the door.

Allegra jumped up before she could talk herself out of it.

'Don't go. Rahim, please don't go.'

He balled his fists and turned from the door. 'What the hell do you want from me, Allegra?'

'For starters, I'd like to feel like I'm not in this alone.' She laced her fingers together, desperately fighting for the words to make him stay. 'I told you my parents died. But I didn't tell you how they died or what my life was like when they were alive.'

He remained silent, and she forced herself to continue.

'My father was a chronic drug abuser and a mean drunk. He was constantly in and out of rehab. Each time he vowed to my mother it would be the last time, but he'd relapse within days, sometimes within hours. And they fought, all the time. Living with them was like living in a constant war zone.'

Rahim frowned. 'You're close to your grandfather. Where was he when this was happening?'

She shrugged, the weight of her childhood drowning her. 'He was around, and he did everything he could, but even at five I knew there was only so much anyone could do. I was six when I watched my mother get into my father's car to stop him leaving after he'd been drinking. They were screaming at each other when he drove away. That was the last time I saw either of them alive.'

The teardrop that landed on her hand was the first indication that she was crying. Scrunching her features to stem the torrent, she jerked as Rahim loomed in front of her. He stared at her for several seconds, the hard look on his face not dissipating.

'Why are you telling me this?'

'I told you in Geneva I didn't think I'd make a good mother. I still don't. And you not being here terrifies me even more.'

His frown deepened. 'But why does your childhood experience write you off as good parent material?'

Allegra reared back. 'Are you serious? I have the DNA of a chronic drug addict and a highly strung mother who could barely take care of herself, let alone her seven kids, running through my veins. Not to mention my every attempt to hold my family together after they were gone ended in disaster. Dysfunctional doesn't begin to describe my family both before and after my parents died. Everything I tried to do made things worse. And you think I should blithely waltz into parenthood?'

'That's exactly the point. You're wealthy enough to follow in your parents' decadent footsteps, and yet you haven't. You chose a different path for yourself. And as for holding your family together, I'm sorry to break it to you, but six-year-olds can barely tie their shoelaces, let alone undertake the monumental task of holding a family together.'

Allegra blinked. She'd unveiled her sordid parentage and

childhood to Rahim. And he'd barely blinked at the monumental fear that had ruled her life since she was six years
old. She didn't know whether to be hurt or thankful that
he'd all but dismissed her fears as inconsequential. Had she
blown her inability to help her siblings all out of proportion? Recalling her grandfather stating something similar,
she closed her eyes and laid her hand over her belly. Had
she really been unrealistic in thinking she was responsible
for holding her family together at such a young age? And
dared she believe that she could do a better job as a mother?

Any hope that might have dared to grow died at the
thought of doing this alone. 'I know that. I'm not stupid,
Rahim. We had nannies and housekeepers to help, but I
had a duty to my family too. And yet nothing I did as I
got older helped. I have zero confidence that I'll be able
to give my child anything worth a damn. What guaran-
tees do I have that I won't ruin his life?' she asked bleakly.

That stopped him for a moment. Then his lips pursed.
'First of all, this is *our* child. Secondly, there are *no* guar-
antees. And you forget, you won't be alone in that, Allegra. This is my child too. He will have the benefit of
two parents.'

'You expect me to believe that when you swing by for
a few hours, then take off again?'

A thunderous frown clamped his brows. 'I have work
to do. You know the extent of what needs to be fixed for
my people.'

'*Our* people, Rahim. We're married, remember? They're
my people too now.'

'Then you should understand…'

'Is it what happened with your mother that's keeping
you away? Or me?'

'Allegra,' he warned.

'What happened on our wedding night wasn't your
fault.'

He went rigid, his features hard as stone. Encouraged that she was getting a reaction, she approached. When he didn't turn away from her, she laid a hand on his chest.

Firming her resolve, she blurted out what she'd been waiting almost a whole day to say to him. 'What happened to your mother was horrible and devastating. But millions of women deliver babies safely every year. Our baby will be too.'

'This palace ceased to be a place of fairy tale a long time ago. You can't flick a magic wand and have everything go your way. The Dar-Amanian people need me. Serving their needs isn't a job I take lightly. We must all make sacrifices for the greater good.'

Feeling like a pathetic heel but knowing she needed to fight for this, she cupped his jaw. 'I didn't sign up for a life of loneliness in a gilded cage, Rahim, greater good or not.'

He glanced sharply at her. 'What are you saying?'

'I want you to come back. I want my husband, my sheikh, to come back to me.' She took another step closer, trapping him between the door and her body.

A shudder moved through him, lifting his chest against hers. Reaching up with her other hand, she cradled his face in her hands, rose on tiptoes and kissed him.

With a guttural groan, he captured her hips and dragged her closer, his touch burning through the flimsy clinic gown. His mouth feasted on hers, biting and lapping, until they were both panting.

'Come back to me, please. I need you, Rahim,' she pleaded.

He gave a groan and her heart lifted.

But in the next breath, he was pulling away. Desperately, she clung to him. 'Don't leave me again. Please!'

'No. The baby...'

'He's fine and healthy. So am I. But we both need you.' She pressed her mouth to his, and they clashed once again in a frenzied exchange of pent-up sexual need. Locking her fingers in his hair, Allegra strained against him, her senses on fire, her heart offering up every prayer it could for the love of her life to stay.

But once again he dragged himself away.

She held her breath as Rahim stared down at her. Silently, she willed him to give her something. She'd pleaded. She'd demanded. She wasn't too far off tears, and she wasn't sure her heart could withstand another rejection.

But it could lurch wildly. And it did when Rahim took her wrists in his hands and determinedly pulled her hands from his face.

'No. This *cannot* happen.'

Her heart in tatters, she stepped away, removing herself from his path. 'Go, then. But don't expect me to be here when you come back.'

His eyes darkened until they were almost black. 'I'm disappointed you feel that way,' he said stonily.

He walked away, leaving her broken and defeated against the wall.

CHAPTER THIRTEEN

RAHIM BARELY MADE it to the guest suite before his legs gave out. He'd taken a secret staircase to evade his bodyguards and to prevent being caught up in the royal baby fever sweeping the palace and Dar-Aman.

His bodyguards would find him eventually—they were too efficiently trained not to—but for now he had a few minutes to himself. A few minutes to replay Allegra's words. A few minutes to lose his mind.

There'd been a time when he would've shrugged off a woman's threat to leave him.

But she wasn't just any woman. This was Allegra, proud woman of breeding.

His wife. His queen.

Stumbling to the well-stocked bar, he poured himself a drink from a bottle whose label he didn't read. The drink was bracing, so he poured himself another. His hand froze halfway to his mouth.

Allegra had never made an idle threat. He'd followed her new foundation's progress for the past few weeks. Each time a course of action was curtailed or bureaucratic red tape thrown up, she found another way. Each time she came up against a male opponent who made the mistake of underestimating her, she promised to get her way. And she did.

He slammed the drink on the bar and caught his head in his hands. His wife had begged him to stay, to work on a marriage he'd pushed on her in the first place. And he'd answered her by walking away like a coward. She was carrying his child, a baby for whom her heart shone through her eyes.

Slowly he lifted his head. If he wasn't mistaken he'd caught a trace of that same look for *him* in her eyes. Even if he was mistaken and dreamed up scenarios that weren't there, every doctor he'd seen regarding Allegra's and their baby's health had told him the same thing—the likelihood of something going wrong was low. He'd listened to the advice but he hadn't believed, not deep down.

All he'd been able to recall was the blood and Allegra's screams when she'd thought she was losing their son. But she had rallied.

He'd hurt her deeply. And she'd stayed, giving of herself to whomever asked, loving his people. Perhaps even loving him?

His heart jumped.

His phone beeped. Tugging it from his pocket, he flung it on the counter without looking at the screen. His mind was sifting through the expressions he'd seen on Allegra's face.

Each one made him hope a little more...

The phone beeped again. About to fling it across the room, he glanced at the message. With a dark curse, he sprinted for the door.

He arrived in the royal suite ninety seconds later. The room was impeccably neat. And deathly quiet.

Panic flared through him. 'Allegra? Allegra!' When his voice echoed back to him, he dug frantically for his phone. Each second felt like a year before his head of security picked up.

'She's not here! Where is she?' he demanded, his soul tearing in two. 'Well, she's not here. Watch the gates. And don't let her leave!'

His grip tight around the phone, he turned to lunge back out the door.

'Don't let who leave?'

Rahim whirled around, his heart banging wildly against his ribs at the sight of Allegra framed in the dressing room doorway. Behind her, clothes were strewn on the floor and two suitcases stood open. He didn't think twice before he acted. Racing to the door, he slammed it shut and turned the key in the lock. Taking it out, he closed his fist over it, hard enough to cause him pain.

'Don't let who leave, Rahim?' she demanded again. Her voice was a husky croak.

'You, Allegra. My bodyguards alerted me that you'd summoned a car to take you to the airport. I told them not to let you leave.'

Her pain-soaked eyes went from his closed fist to the door. 'And you think a locked door is going to stop me?'

He shook his head, his breath coming in pants as fear rode his very soul. 'No, nothing can stop you when you set your mind to something. I know that now. I don't deserve the time of day from you, but I hope you'll give me a chance to let me take away the hurt that I've caused you.' He crossed the room and gently took her hand. Turning her palm up, he dropped the key into it and curled her fingers closed.

Then he cast another glance into the dressing room, and almost broke down at her feet. With every fibre of his being, Rahim wanted to move her away from the scene where she was preparing to leave him. But he forced himself to stay rooted to the floor.

Her nostrils flared slightly before her mouth compressed. 'Five minutes. Then I'm out the door.'

Rahim swallowed hard. 'I've been running scared ever since my mother died. You know what happened to her.'

Sympathy shadowed her face before she nodded. 'Complications during the birth of your brother?'

'Yes, but what you probably don't know is that the complications could've been avoided. She had me by emergency Caesarean section after a complicated labour which she barely survived. When she was diagnosed with placenta praevia for her second pregnancy, she was told the child would most likely have to be delivered by Caesarean section too. But somewhere along the line, she got it into her head that she could deliver naturally. Nothing her doctors said would sway her. She was fragile and naturally petite, with her head always in the clouds. As a child, she used to fascinate me. I couldn't quite believe I came from this almost mythical creature, but I loved her all the same. And she loved me. Of course, my father's intense love for her wasn't a secret. There was nothing he wouldn't do for her, including not standing in the way of the sometimes questionable decisions she would make. The first time I heard them row was over her decision about the baby. He begged her to have the Caesarean. She point-blank refused. He told her he wouldn't be able to go on if something happened and he lost her.

'I was hiding in this very dressing room when he said that to her. I remember dismissing the statement as utter nonsense. Loving a person shouldn't involve a death pledge or disagreements that led to blazing rows. But with each refusal, my father promised her he wouldn't live if she died. A month later, she went into labour. Her stubborn belief that she could do it naturally eventually put the child in distress. By the time the doctors took action, there was too much blood loss and she was too frail to survive the Caesarean. The baby died, and so did she.'

Allegra's face twisted in agony for him. 'Rahim, I'm so sorry,' she whispered.

'And just as he'd promised, my father stopped living.

He just…turned everything off.' Remembered bitterness pounded through him, the pain relentless as he lived it all over again. 'Nothing I did or said made a difference, and believe me, I did everything I could imagine, savoury *and* unsavoury. Sadly, the unsavoury bits lingered long after I'd attempted to turn over a new leaf.'

'Possibly because you enjoyed your wild side a little bit too much?' She didn't exactly tease as she said it, and Rahim wondered if that would be yet another mark against him.

'I was desperate. I'd gone from a pampered and loved child to losing two parents in one day, even though only one of them died.'

'But you were lucky—you knew love for a while before it was taken away. No matter how devastating that was, you still have good memories to hang on to.' She looked away, her eyes darkening with her own pain. Pain that lashed at Rahim. She turned and headed back into the dressing room. Rahim followed, resisting the urge to shut and bolt that door too. 'Mine died as they lived, in a fiery blaze of glory,' she continued. 'With barely a thought for their seven children. Had it not been for my grandfather none of us would be where we are today.'

'That's why you risked everything for him.'

'I love him. I would do anything for him.'

'Even marry a man you barely know so your grandfather could keep his treasured box?'

She stiffened for a second, then bent to pick up a discarded garment. Disconsolately, she tossed it into a suitcase. 'Why are you doing this, Rahim? You don't want to be married to me. I got the message loud and clear today. So let's just save ourselves this unnecessary post-mortem. I've no more of my heart to pour out.'

She bent down to pick up another bunch of clothes. Rahim lunged for them, wrestled them from her. 'And I haven't poured my heart out enough. So let's redress the balance.'

Allegra froze, her stunning blue eyes searching his for a frantic second before she shook her head. 'You *know* what love is, Rahim. You feel it for this baby. I know you do. So please believe me when I say I won't stop my child from experiencing that love. And I won't publicise any separation until he's old enough…'

'No!' The word tore free from his chest, a lifetime of hopeless fear rising up to choke him, sending him to his knees. He wrapped his hands around her waist and pleaded for his life. 'Please, *ya galbi*, no separation. No divorce. I'll do whatever it takes. I was a coward, too afraid to admit what I felt for you until now. I don't want to say "until it was too late," because I don't want it to be. I would reverse time itself if I could to redress all the wrong turns I've taken. Please let us not be one of them. Tell me what you want me to do and I'll do it. Please, Allegra. I love you. Don't leave me.'

She gasped, her eyes flaring wide as she stared down at him. 'You love me,' she muttered obliquely.

'I love you,' he affirmed. 'I feared that love would make me weak as it did my father. When you bled on our wedding night, I nearly lost my mind with the terror of imagining losing you. I mistakenly thought being without you was better than falling deeper in love with you to the point where I wouldn't be able to function. But I recognise the difference between what my parents had and what I feel for you. Being with you empowers me to be better, to do better for my people. And I don't love you any less by staying away from you.'

'Oh, Rahim.'

'So given the choice between shutting myself off in some godforsaken remote location in my kingdom or seeing you every day, watching our son grow in your belly…

habibi, the choice is very simple. I want to love you, up close and as personal as you'll allow me.'

'I want it very personal, Rahim. As personal as you showed me it could be on our wedding night. I want that every day and every night.' Her eyes filled with tears until they spilled from her glorious lashes onto his face. Laughing, she brushed them away, then lowered her mouth to his. 'Promise me that, and you'll have my love forever.'

Rahim's heart raced, his soul baring itself to the fierce love shining from her eyes. 'I promise. You honour me with your love.'

'And my body and soul.'

'And I honour you with mine, my Allegra. Forever.'

They kissed, reverently, then hungrily, before she pulled away. Slowly she opened her hand. 'I think we should use this now.'

'Is there somewhere special you'd like me to take you?'

'Yes, please. I'd like to finish our wedding night in the tent. Then I'd like to go to Long Island. There's a grandfather there who needs to know he's about to become a great-grandfather in a few short months.'

Rahim took the key from her and caught her hand in his. 'Your wish, my dear heart, is my command.'

Nabil Giovanni Al-Hadi was born two weeks shy of his due date. His premature entry into the world sent his parents, uncles and aunts around the world into a tailspin. But his great-grandfather, in whose presence he was born, took it all in his stride.

The day her grandfather held his first great-grandson, Allegra Al-Hadi burst into happy tears. How could she ever have doubted how powerful love could be? How giving and life-affirming in every way?

Rahim had agreed for them to try for another baby and she couldn't wait.

Nothing held a more special, sacred duty for her than to fill the Dar-Aman Palace with its future princes and princesses, hone them into fine citizens who would treasure their kingdom as much as she and Rahim did.

'You're crying and smiling at the same time, *ya habibi*. Should I be worried?' Rahim asked as he entered her childhood room in the Di Sione mansion on Long Island. They'd agreed to divide their family time between Long Island and Dar-Aman because they didn't know how much time Giovanni had. With the kingdom thriving once more, it had been an easy decision to make.

'I was thinking about the future and the endless possibilities for our children.'

Rahim shrugged out of his robe and approached where she lay in bed. His naked, honed body sent hers into fever pitch, and his loving but arrogant expression told her he knew it. 'If you want Nabil to have six siblings too, then we need to get started on the next one.'

Allegra laughed as she went into her husband's arms. 'Yes, my sheikh.'

And he proceeded to show her just how earth-shattering their love could be.

* * * * *

If you enjoyed this book,
look out for the next instalment of
THE BILLIONAIRE'S LEGACY:
TO BLACKMAIL A DI SIONE
by Rachael Thomas.
Coming next month.

MILLS & BOON®

MODERN™

POWER, PASSION AND IRRESISTIBLE TEMPTATION

0816/01

MILLS & BOON®

The Regency Collection – Part 1

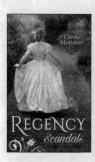

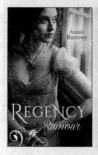
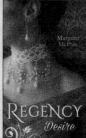

Let these roguish rakes sweep you off to the
Regency period in part 1 of our collection!

Order yours at **www.millsandboon.co.uk/regency1**

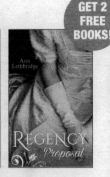

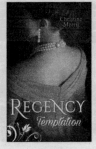